# HAPPINESS AND LOVE

*A Novel*

## ZOE DUBNO

SCRIBNER

NEW YORK   AMSTERDAM/ANTWERP   LONDON
TORONTO   SYDNEY/MELBOURNE   NEW DELHI

Scribner

An Imprint of Simon & Schuster, LLC

1230 Avenue of the Americas

New York, NY 10020

First Scribner hardcover edition September 2025

SCRIBNER and design are trademarks of Simon & Schuster, LLC

Simon & Schuster strongly believes in freedom of expression and stands against censorship in all its forms. For more information, visit BooksBelong.com.

For information about special discounts for bulk purchases, please contact Simon & Schuster Special Sales at 1-866-506-1949 or business@simonandschuster.com.

The Simon & Schuster Speakers Bureau can bring authors to your live event. For more information or to book an event, contact the Simon & Schuster Speakers Bureau at 1-866-248-3049 or visit our website at www.simonspeakers.com.

Interior design by Kathryn A. Kenney-Peterson

Manufactured in the United States of America

10  9  8  7  6  5  4  3  2  1

Library of Congress Control Number: 2025936736

ISBN 978-1-6680-6295-1

ISBN 978-1-6680-6296-8 (ebook)

*for Will*

I was born here and I'll die here, against my will.

—Bob Dylan

While everyone was waiting for the actress to arrive from her premiere, I sat in the corner seat of the white linen sofa at Eugene's with my legs crossed, watching the rest of the party and regretting my decision to attend. I was surrounded by the very people that I had spent the last five years avoiding, people who had taken advantage of the death of our friend Rebecca to drag me back to their cathedral of modernist rococo on the Bowery. I had recently returned to New York, the city of my birth, from London, where I had been living. The decision to return was not mine. I had run out my visas, first in Europe, and then in the UK I had no other option but to return to America for the winter. Only now, as I sat on the sofa, watching Eugene, a man who could reasonably be called one of my closest friends, describe the *materiality* and the *performance* of a set of bookshelves he'd just installed, did I realize that I could have waited out the winter months in Papua New Guinea or China or some other place where I knew nobody and the European and British immigration authorities had no hold over me. I realized now that I would have been better off in Papua New Guinea or China or some other third place. I hadn't seen Eugene or anyone at his party in the five years since I'd left New York for a brief trip to

Rome, a city with its own problems, which I'd soon fled for London. I hadn't told anyone that I was back from London, but then I ran into Eugene that morning when I made the mistake of pacing up and down the Bowery to clear my mind. I was living uptown, but, after Rebecca's mother called to inform me of her death, which had not surprised me but did fling me into a state of something like shock, I felt the need to walk up and down the Bowery the way I did when I was last productive and of sound mind while in New York. I needed to be pacing up and down the Bowery, that double-wide street, practically the Champs-Élysées of Manhattan, listening to Mozart's Clarinet Concerto on my headphones and avoiding the stares and entreaties of the many crazy people that sat on the ground outside the Bowery Mission as if I were any less crazy than them, pacing back and forth down the Bowery trying to get my mind to start working so I could write. Every time I make plans to travel, I think it is going to be better once I get there and I am settled. In London, I think I am going to be able to write once I am in New York, on the Upper West Side in my grandmother's apartment, sitting at the enormous desk with room for my papers and books and sticky notes, but when I sit down in the imagined seat that would solve all my problems it often does not work, and I need to go and walk up and down some street. When I was in London, I thought that if I could just walk up and down the Bowery, as I used to, I would be able to get some writing done. So, I'd taken the subway downtown and walked up the Bowery to Cooper Square and back down to Chinatown and up to Cooper Square and down to Chinatown. After six or seven passes of the Bowery I began thinking again, first of politics and then my writing and the story I had been working on, and became anxious to get back to my desk uptown. This is helping me, I thought. Walking on the Bowery is helping me. And I chuckled to myself and thought derisively of the people that have ruined the word *flâneur* for those of us who so desperately *need* flânerie in order to exist, those wretched people who have ruined the idea through identification with the flâneur—which they clearly do not understand is *not a subject* but a *literary archetype*, they don't understand that one cannot, simply through their idleness and love of walking, *be* a flâneur. But this is the problem with many people in my generation, who have conditioned themselves to believe that they *are a Samantha*, a Libra, an INFJ, and that this means something important to the rest of us, that this in some way *speaks to their ambitions*, and without realizing it my legs had carried me across Hester Street, on the route I once walked toward my old apartment on Eldridge after figuring everything out on the Bowery. And there, in the middle of Hester Street, when I thought I was safe, thinking peacefully about the story I was writing, momentarily free from thoughts of Rebecca, whom I had not seen in years and had been informed that morning was dead, I was confronted with the door to my favorite lunch café. I decided I could not go in. I could not see the people I knew who sat endlessly in this café, reading the art magazines in its cubic plywood banquettes, eating the bowls of seed butter and vegetable puree, gorging themselves on the baroque, admittedly delicious health food. I wanted to go into the café and have the bright green Mexican soup that I had craved since leaving the city but I knew that I could not under any circumstances enter the café, nor even pause to look at its laser-cut plywood fake Donald Judd interior through the window, because without a doubt people that I knew—the people that I had taken great pains to avoid by keeping the barrier of 72nd to 14th Streets between us, after being forced by the immigration authorities to close the great Atlantic Ocean barrier I had maintained for five years—would be inside. They'd be sucking up their smoothies, listening to whatever music the waitresses, *artists* all, decided to put on, in my experience No Wave or Japanese ambient music or free jazz, to soundtrack the nut-milk-latte drinking, usually some kind of music that was intended to bolster the artistic reputation of the restaurant using the dregs of eighties countercultural signifiers to transform the sale of sulfite-free imported wine into an artistic or moral choice. In fact, it had once been my habit to ask them to turn the music down in the restaurant if I was there, attempting to have a peaceful late-morning coffee and to sit and read their copies of the art magazines that I occasionally wrote for but would never purchase. I often sat inside the restaurant trying to read the pieces that my so-called peers had written, avoiding my own pieces, which I wrote only to pay for my expenses. In retrospect I wish that I had used a pseudonym for those articles— articles about fashion trends and hairstyles and restaurants that I was forced to write to pay for my expenses. Articles about designers and models and their housewares and skin-care routines that I was forced to attach my name to. I wish that I had used a pseudonym. Or I really wish that I had learned to profit off some sort of nobler trade like carpentry or ax-grinding rather than peddling garbage articles to worthless magazines to fill the spaces between automobile advertisements. I wanted to go into the café now, to look at what had become of the magazines and their writers, but I was afraid that the people I once referred to as my friends would be inside. Or, even worse, if they weren't in there, someone who *was* might report my whereabouts to the people I was hiding from, *my friends*, which, from my perch on the white linen sofa at Eugene's house, I realized was another great vanity: that I was afraid of being reported on to Eugene and the rest of them when I was now, just the following day, conveyed of my free will, by my own two feet, here in Eugene's apartment, which I had once known so well and had tried to avoid, though clearly not so hard. I stopped short just outside the café and turned around on Hester to head back to the Bowery. As I moved to conceal myself from the café, I laughed to myself, thinking that of course *I* was not a flâneur but, much more appropriately, I was Proust's *passante*, a fugitive woman forced to walk briskly and covertly through my own city, and as I had this thought, which also as I thought it made me sick, because of course this thought is no different from *I am a Samantha*, and is actually *much worse* than that thought, for obvious reasons, as I spun around to walk back down Hester toward the Bowery, I found myself standing face-to-face with the bushy eyebrows and delicate nose of Eugene, who, without saying hello, without offering the most basic greeting, asked if I had been back in New York for a long time. Because I am a pathetic coward, eager to please even the people I most detest, I lied and said that I had only returned the day before when in reality, of course, I had returned weeks before our meeting, and what I should have said is that I had returned weeks before our meeting and that I did not tell him or anyone else that I had returned because I had no intention of seeing him or any of the people that crowded around his apartment for his *evenings*—his *evenings* where people who called themselves *artists* and *directors* but in fact worked as *content creators* and *creative directors* made a mockery of themselves and of the idea of the *artist* and even the idea of the *director* by talking only of the budgets of their films, the net worths of their collectors, and the vacation homes of their producers. But instead, when I was met with the very person I wanted to see least in all of New York, Eugene, the *multidisciplinary artist*, wearing one of his brightly colored outfits, his cobalt beret and enormous shiny yellow jacket—his jackets were always enormous, and did for him, a diminutive balding man, what the bouffant hairstyle did for ugly women—when I saw this ungainly array, because I always have been spineless and a coward, rather than say I'd been back for weeks and didn't want to see him, instead I said that I had just arrived on last night's red-eye flight, a red-eye flight that in fact had gotten in that very morning. And so, I recalled, as I sat in the corner seat of Eugene's white Restoration Hardware sofa that I remembered had actually been purchased in beige but, once it crossed the threshold of his home he had realized was *all wrong*, so he had it slipcovered in white linen, which I had to admit, as I looked around at the apartment that I'd been away from for so long, really did suit the place better than beige, that when I was standing on the street with Eugene, wishing that I'd carried an umbrella to hide my face behind and he asked me to attend his *little dinner* the very next evening with *everyone*, his dinner that he was giving to celebrate an actress that I will *probably have heard of,* because I am a coward, I said that I had no other plans. That of course I would love nothing more than to *see all the old faces.* He was standing next to the door of the café, and I began to worry that someone even worse, though I'm not sure who that could be, would come out of the door, so I lunged forward to begin walking. Eugene took this as an invitation to walk with me along Hester Street back toward the Bowery, and as we walked he slung his large orange tote bag over his shoulder, stuffed full of what he called *texts to fuel his study of object-oriented ontology,* which he had just bought *new, foolishly,* at McNally Jackson, though he knew he could *find them second-hand,* he just *could not wait,* before having a little *solo lunch* at the café. *If I hadn't stopped to have a little power bowl,* he said, with what I could tell was the utmost pleasure, *I would never have run into you.* He flashed me his perverted little smile, the corners of his eyes scrunching up into crow's-feet, his salt-and-pepper stubble wrinkling around his dimples. Then suddenly I saw this perverted smile twist into what I am sure was supposed to be a solemn face pregnant with gravitas. *I*—here he paused and looked at his feet—*I almost forgot to ask you if you knew about*

*Rebecca*, he said, affecting a change in his voice but without slowing the pace of our walk, which had sped up as if we were trying to outrun one another. *Your American phone line has been off all this time, all the texts deliver in that green way or not at all, so I would think no one would have been able to reach you.* I asked him what he meant by *about Rebecca*, knowing full well that she had died of a drug overdose in her parents' home on the coast of Massachusetts because her mother had called to tell me a few days earlier through her Boston-accented tears. *She passed*, Eugene said, pausing now on the Bowery. *She's dead, her mother called me to tell me that she passed.* Eugene saying that she had *passed* confused me, as *passed* sounded to me like an incredibly Christian way of describing death, *passed* implying that she had *passed into a better place*, and I felt disoriented because Eugene was such a godless person and so I looked confused or maybe shocked when he said it, even though I already knew that she was dead, which gave Eugene the satisfaction of thinking he'd been able to tell me that she had died. *I'm sure her mother was planning on calling you*, he said, *you were close too.* I didn't correct him. I didn't want to participate in the crude and pathetic game that people like to play with the dead, making out like they were the only one that was *truly close* to the dead person—the dead person, who *while they were living* was no more than shit off the shoe to them, suddenly becomes *their dearest friend*, suddenly they are the *only person* that needs to be told that they have died—so I allowed him the satisfaction of thinking that he had been the one to break the horrible news to me, to surprise me in the middle of the most decrepit part of the Bowery with the death of our friend Rebecca, though I was not in the least surprised when I heard from her mother that she had died; I was surprised only that it had taken so long for her to concoct a sufficiently lethal cocktail of narcotics. I was not sure if the death was by suicide or by accident, but when one consumes as many pills as Rebecca, it's hard to find the line where an overdose ceases to be an accident and becomes a suicide. And so while I was in my state of so-called shock about Rebecca's death, which was really a state of perturbance, perturbance that I had once again allowed the idiot Eugene to get the best of me, I accepted his invitation to this dreadful dinner at his *floor-through loft* apartment on the Bowery, the *floor-through loft* that I had known so well for so long, where I now sat, having been successfully lured to this dinner party *in honor of an actress* who was now hours late. And of course, it had played to my vanity when Eugene told me that everyone *would really be excited to see me*, I thought, as I watched Eugene's *partner* Nicole, her thick legs wrapped in a long purple skirt, pour too much red wine into her glass, greedily making sure she *had enough*, just as she always had. I have noticed that the rich are the most concerned with making sure they get their *fair share*. Eugene was wealthy, the son of a successful and genuinely talented artist. Their *floor-through loft* was once his studio. But Nicole was the really rich one, the daughter of a *financier*, as she called him, and his art-collector third wife. When I had just left college and moved back to the city and crossed the threshold of this *floor-through loft* for the first time, I immediately knew that I'd entered a completely different city from the one that I had grown up in. A new-world *downtown*, a place full of *artists* and *critics*, and once I entered it, I forgot about everything I'd done, everyone I'd known before. I had rapidly become friends with Nicole and Eugene and their group, the same group I now watched eating beluga caviar on *marcelled* potato chips, the kitsch, appetizing specialty *de la maison* marrying *high* and *low*, from which I abstained from my perch on the sofa. I remembered that when I had first fallen in with this group I had gone by myself to a gallery to see the work of an artist named Ymelda Garros, and I had remarked to Nicole that I had loved the sculptures at the show, that I was amazed by the sculptures at the show, which were small and yellow and childlike though somehow still sleek, and as I began to relate this to Nicole, she cut me off to say that it was *EEE-melda* not *Yeh-melda*. And she shook her head and made a face that she often made, a horrible puckered-up face of disgust that she also made when you were shopping with her and picked a blouse that she thought was not in good taste, and I repeated the name correctly this time, oh, *EEE-melda*, and this was enough. She nodded her head and smiled, and then began to talk about something else. She did not want me to continue to tell her what I had thought about the art, or rather, it was completely irrelevant to her what the sculpture looked like, meant, or was, because I had learned the correct way to say the name of the artist. The meaning but also the image and form of the art was of no consequence. The correct pronunciation of Ymelda Garros was of sublime importance, however, which I would later learn was because Nicole's mother owned six of the artist's sculptures. They were littered around her family's houses in Rhinebeck and Montauk like they were clock radios or umbrella stands, and to mispronounce the artist's name was to devalue the importance of the investment, an investment that was of course a pittance compared to the total sum of Nicole's future inheritance from her mother. And so when the name was properly said, then the Ymelda Garros affair was over, because it was so incredibly banal to her. It was like correctly pronouncing the word *toothbrush*. It is noteworthy only that it has been mispronounced, but after it is corrected there is no need to go on talking about the toothbrush. In this way the rich, through their ownership of art, not only soil the piece for themselves, by adding it to their hoard and reducing the work of art to an object like a clock radio, but also ruin it for all who attempt to enjoy the piece because they so often believe that they, the owners, are the sole authority on the work, the only ones who can *truly understand it*. They believe that by *purchasing the work*, that in exchange for *handing over the cash*, they receive from the artist not only the piece but also the key to *what it means*, but of course they never do understand the work, they are the people that understand the work least in the world, they are the destroyers of the work. And though there are so many ways that the rich can destroy the art that they buy—licensing it to fashion brands and tech ads, cluttering their walls to create a disgusting mismatched gallery of their hoard—Nicole had destroyed her collection in the worst way, the way that rich people with good taste and with artist friends destroy their purchases. In a rapture of cognitive dissonance they love *great art* but derive great shame from hoarding artwork, they are *embarrassed by their riches* so they *lock their art away* in storage so that their addiction to accumulation—and, more importantly, their taste—can never be commented on. Of course Nicole's job was to have taste in art, but in her job as an art curator she could always say that she had *made an acquisition* because it *made sense for the museum*. In her own art collecting, her own *art buying*, she was much more private, worried that the large sum she spent on some piece would make too big a statement about what she herself valued, leaving her open for ridicule, for judgment or, *quelle horreur*, legibility. Then, eight or so years ago, I did not yet know that there were an untold number of *pieces* locked away in Nicole's collection, mostly old master paintings her father had hidden from her mother in a free port in Geneva during their divorce, the knowledge of which may have diminished the feeling of joy I felt when I got a smile from Nicole for saying *EEE-melda* correctly, a smile that at that time I wanted so desperately, a genuine smile from this woman over a decade my senior who at the time was the very center of my universe, who I believed was also the very center of the *genuine vibrant artistic universe*, which I had previously thought was nonextant. The only access I had had to vibrant artistic worlds was through elderly academics in college and Renaissance paintings at the Met, and the world that created these things no longer existed, these were figures from a *period of art history*; contemporary art had never interested me because of the narrative of *decay* that was presented to us endlessly in New

York, the *shuttering* of CBGB, the over-institutionalization of MoMA, the CIA's invention of modernism, the rising rents all around the city that had made the world depicted in seventies cinema and the books of Kathy Acker unattainable to the current generation, Fran Lebowitz's interminable bloviation about New York City's demise. But when I met Nicole and Eugene, the curator and the photographer couple who took me into their little group and their world there on the Bowery, I felt for the first time like it was possible for me to make art and to be surrounded by an *artistic community* of *real artists*, to not feel embarrassed by my *artistic aspirations* and to meet others that were serious about their *art*. Whenever Nicole smiled at me her status as a curator made it feel like she was saying *you are a real artist*, and because of that I loved her so desperately. Now her smile makes me want to get up and run, I thought, sitting on the sofa in her home, her smile tells me I'm a disgusting person, that I've allowed my vigilance to slip and I've followed my worst instincts to the basement of society. It is astounding how at one time we can be so desperate for the approval of a beloved friend, we can debase ourselves in pursuit of the approval and love that we crave and feel we are so cruelly denied, until suddenly when our labors have paid off and we are granted this love, the feeling of friendship and comfort that was once so *elusive and desired* becomes repulsive to us. It becomes absolutely disgusting to us, I thought, as I sat on the white linen sofa, watching Nicole speak to Alexander, gesticulating with her hands in the way that she had learned from the elderly proprietor of a terrible café on the Lower East

Side, the worst café imaginable, that Nicole insisted was the greatest restaurant in the city, for the sole reason that the proprietor—a wretched, charmless old man—paid attention to her. She would propose that café as the meeting point for any lunch, even though the food was dreadful—the only thing I trusted on the laminated placard he had the *chutzpah* to call a *menu* was a can of tuna fish with store-bought mayonnaise mixed directly into the tin—but she would say *don't you just love it here* and of course you had no option but to agree that you did, until suddenly, one afternoon when I had accompanied Nicole and Rebecca to the café and I took a sip of my coffee and got grounds in my teeth, I finally lost it and told Nicole what I really thought of the café. I lost it and told her what I thought of her thick manicured fingers imitating the gestures of the Brooklyn-accented proprietor, and of the brainless exhibitions she curated about the intersection of this and that and the other thing, about the way that she was an intellectual bottom-feeder, trawling the *ocean floor* to scavenge ideas so stale, so old, so *obvious*, ideas that had been chewed over by so many idiots that they'd become totally meaningless, ideas that had traveled from the surface, from whatever *theory* she had half read and not understood, ricocheted off the *intellectuals* she thought she was friends with and met at Davos, and wound up at the bottom of the ocean floor, they had in fact reached the *bottom of the Mariana Trench*, and only then would Nicole understand these ideas, only then would Nicole pick up these ideas and use them in her exhibitions, these sad pathetic worn-out ideas. And that *everyone who went to her exhibitions knew this*, except for her, *everyone knew* that her thematic choices were legible yet totally incoherent, *zeitgeisty* and pathetically stale, and I told her what I thought of her *partner* and their *house upstate* and the *chickens* and the antique tractor she wanted to buy as Rebecca stroked her arm gently, consoling her, while looking straight at me, repressing a smile. And as I thought of Rebecca's big eyes, eternally rimmed with smeary black kohl, I felt my own eyes begin to water, and I promised myself to not think about Rebecca or else I would be forced to cry in front of these people. I have never been able to control my tears. Looking at Nicole, I was amazed again that I had once craved her love so desperately, since now even the sight of her made me want to jump straight out of my skin. It made me jealous of the rattlesnake. She had become an absolute allergen to me; seeing her reminded me of when I'd pleaded for her attention and approval, it reminded me of the worthlessness and humiliation of the years of my sycophantic behavior, which I should not be forgiven for even if I was nineteen and touched to be taken seriously as an artist by people that I believed I should admire. It hurt to be reminded that Nicole, the curator, and her *partner* Eugene, the *photographer* and *multimedia artist*, once held such a special place for me. That must be why, I thought as I sat on my seat on their sofa, that must be why so many people cannot extricate themselves from Eugene's and Nicole's lives. Even if they have outgrown them, even if, once they have learned the true character of Eugene and Nicole, they no longer care for them, even if they outright despise them, it is too painful to *draw a line under the years*

*they spent worshipping them*, it is too painful to admit to yourself
that you have been a complete fool for so long. And so they elevate Eugene and Nicole *further*, they make them even more inte-
gral to their lives, they introduce them to all of their friends,
they name their children after them, they go to Greece together,
because that is the only way to avoid the realization that so much
of their lives has been a lie. Of course, my admiration for Eugene
and Nicole was won because of my ability to be willfully blind to
the reality of their situation. I didn't know then that the reason
Eugene and Nicole had access to this world was that Eugene's
father, the famous artist, who was lucky enough to be dead before his son came of age and began his *artistic career* in earnest,
had left them with the *connections and allure* to draw all the *great
thinkers* and *artistic people* into their stylish home on the Bowery,
while Nicole had the money to make their *little evenings* into genuinely attractive events, respites from the world of plastic cups of
acrid Chardonnay and increasingly mediocre gallery dinners. At
these evenings there would be cases of *natural wine* and expensive but understated local-organic-pasture-raised-snout-to-tail-
vegan food that Nicole would pretend to have cooked—but,
from living with them for a year when I had first moved back to
New York and couldn't afford my own apartment, I knew was
catered by a rotating host of pretty chefs who Nicole would call
*chefs in residence* and said *changed seasonally* to explain their short
tenure at the house but who would really quit because they
couldn't bear the constant sexual advances from Eugene—and
we all thought we were indebted to these great benefactors who

fed us, provided us with comfort, and occasionally housed us in their many extra bedrooms, but we were all, the attendees of this *little evening* and of every other *little evening* they put on, we were all victims. Willing and supplicant victims of Eugene and Nicole, who forced us to debase ourselves constantly to thank them for their generosity, generosity bestowed on us in exchange for our legitimizing presence—a stay in the beautiful farmhouse in Rhinebeck in exchange for our smiling faces plastered all over Nicole's Instagram feed, our seats at dinner, which cost a light debate about politics and aesthetics and also the unspoken promise to eventually yield and agree with them, a price that included lending them the credibility that came from our art making, to hand over our thoughts and ideas in exchange for a *free escape from the city* in the middle of a *sweltering August*, to simply hand over our inner thoughts, the material of our artistic practice, the essence of our lives, in exchange for this *free* retreat, our thoughts and ideas that would of course furnish Nicole's exhibitions and show up in Eugene's commercial photography. If you were a painter, he would *invite you up*, maybe even buy one of your *pictures*, and weeks later you'd see he'd taken a photo for a fashion ad that framed the model the exact same way as you'd framed the subject of your painting. If you were a conceptual artist, you would stay up all night with him drinking his Japanese whiskey and doing his drugs, having one of the more interesting conversations about your work, a conversation that left you feeling validated in your methods, endeared to Eugene, who had really engaged with you on a deep and serious level. You'd leave

Rhinebeck revivified, inspired, and ready to produce something new, only to later discover that Eugene had in fact expertly mined you for your theoretical influences and then employed them in his photography, having first sapped them of any transgressive, innovative, or *interesting* meaning, hacking them into their bare aesthetic parts. Actually, that skill was one of the foundational elements of Eugene's personality, he had been doing it for decades, his career was in fact based on it. He once told me about a time before I knew him when he was close friends with a famous land-artist friend of his father's; he had known him from a young age and the land artist was somewhat of a mentor to him. Eugene had been advised by the land artist for many years about what books to read, what films to watch, what parties to go to, and then—after Eugene's first few minor group shows, at galleries that Eugene's father and the land artist both showed with—as is the course of many young artists' careers, Eugene was offered a gig creative directing a *fashion film*, and rather than declining as the land artist advised Eugene to do in order to protect his artistic integrity if not forever then for a few more years at the very least, rather than declining, Eugene directed the *fashion film* for Gucci set among rusted pipes in the desert. I had never met the land artist and I understood why. He had the good sense, and of course the power, not to rely on Eugene and Nicole's loft on the Bowery, I thought as I sat on the corner seat of the sofa. Though Eugene relied on him for ideas, the land artist did not need his and Nicole's houses or their books or their wine as Rebecca and I had, I thought as I looked at all the interestingly dressed, clever sponges who sat around me in the *conversational area* of Nicole and Eugene's loft on the Bowery. It only took me a few years of being bamboozled by Nicole and Eugene to realize that the entire *artistic world* that they had fashioned for themselves, a world that I had no doubt been enticed by, was a system even worse than the old model of patronage. At least the court artists knew where they stood with their noble benefactors. They were employees, they were servants, and their masters required art from them, entertainment, and in turn the masters bathed in the artist's prestige, they were practicing their duty of *noblesse oblige*, they plied you with wine and food and luxury in order to take credit for fostering your artistic achievements, and they were proud to have financed them, but they were not, as Eugene was, listening to everything you said in order to transform your thoughts and ideas into their commercial artwork, their advertising campaigns for corporations that contained the signature elements of their protégés' artwork laundered to become more palatable for the corporations that required the advertisements to rehabilitate their reputations. Something about Eugene's bloodsuckery made me feel sorry for him. Unlike his silly and cruel *partner,* Eugene was cursed with being both talentless and wise, and this fatal combination of lack of talent and excess of cleverness had driven him to ruin, though not of course professional or financial ruin—his photographs hang in MoMA—but the ruin of his soul, his flight toward alcoholism and drug abuse, his unbridled lechery, and his sad, no-fun debauchery, all made possible only because of his excellent taste and his knowledge that he does not have the ability or the genius to create anything interesting. But because he is a wily man, born into the cradle of the 1970s artistic scene, sired by one of the decade's foremost artists and surrounded since birth by the greatest geniuses of that time, everything was stacked against him. The children of great, genuinely great, artists, unless they manage to outstrip their parents—which, though it has happened in recent years, is incredibly rare—have as options only: to reject the desire to *make something of themselves* and to dedicate their lives to maintaining the reputation and the works of the parent; to rebel by casting off art completely to worship at the altar of financial capital and political power, besting their brilliant parent in monetary terms, while alienating the beloved, brilliant parent, who likely will never consider the accumulation of money and property to be that impressive; or, as is more and more common, to become an artist destined to mimic the tastes, the styles, and the interests of their talented and innovative parent, which worked marvelously in the earlier artistic periods, as in the Renaissance, when Yada Yada the Younger carried out the aesthetic goals of the father under whose guidance he'd worked since early childhood, perhaps eventually besting him technically, but nevertheless leaving a record that allows art history to understand that the father's hand can be seen in the paintings of his more illustrious son, but it is nearly impossible to achieve this joint reputation now, as artistic movements are now measured by the decade rather than the century. The father can teach his son about his own craft, not as something to mimic, but mostly as art history, which of course helps in the formation of an artist's mind but does not give the child a plan to follow, so that all the artist father can do is impress a way of thinking on his child, which is bound to be difficult to achieve because contemporary art has become less and less about mastering technique and more about the conceptual, the personal, the artist as the central figure of his art. So the father cannot help but mythologize his own childhood, his own prime, and the idea that the art springs directly from his mind, following those circumstances, which becomes difficult for the child to assimilate into her own art *because the circumstances of her childhood*, from which, following the model set by her father, she is meant to draw her artistic inspiration and strength, *are directly influenced by her father's artistic movement.* Her childhood memories *contain her father's art practice.* So unlike the art of her father, which so frequently references his rural-urban-immigrant childhood, his alienation from his surroundings, his discovery of the art that made him beloved and a genius and famous and delivered him into the *realm of culture*, she begins *from this end.* To create her art, she must find an origin, or else risk *directly aping* the work of her father and his movement, which, though it remains interesting to study, *is no longer innovative, experimental, or controversial.* But she is often left stuck fascinated by the generation that her parent was a part of—the former avant-garde, which is now the artistic establishment. The artist father has ceased to be a Young Turk of the artistic world and is instead a member of the comfortable, liberal, artistic bourgeoisie, and so for the child, the association of that "old guard" with her childhood renders any attack leveled against the father's generation by her artistic peers—that antagonism that is the exact condition of the founding of her father's artistic movement—an intolerable wound, an attack on her person. So the artistic child of the great artist who chooses to make art has three further choices, the first being to live in a state of arrested development, doing little more than reliving their avant-garde childhood, churning out Fluxus works in 2002, or rehashing punk aesthetics in their SoHo loft, which is now conveniently located above a Chanel store, completely ignoring the realities of their times and living in direct opposition to the intents and instincts of the artists that they are *inspired by*, intents and instincts of which they are *totally unaware*, because of course these artists are *old friends of the family* who have *known them since they were babies* and they themselves *tend also to have lost touch completely with what is going on* in the world outside of New York–LA–Basel–Paris–London and, increasingly, Dubai although they wear beaten-up sneakers to their career retrospectives at MoMA. They also have the choice to exchange their parent's intellectual gifts for mass appeal, like Paloma Picasso did by labeling her fashion brand's perfume Minotaure after the surrealist journal that her father contributed to, which I discovered when I was trying to find an issue of the journal with an early Bataille poem on eBay but could only find dozens of bottles of her nineties perfume branded with the same font as the journal, a journal that most people will never have heard of; so the title and dashed-off red lettering of the journal that published Lacan and Giacometti, because of this child of Picasso, have been immortalized as a vanilla-and-bergamot eau de parfum. Which makes me wonder about Picasso the Younger's Tiffany jewelry, though perhaps jewelry is different than her drugstore perfume, as I am reminded that there has been a *marriage of art and fashion*, to use the title of a show that Nicole curated at the Whitney. The most difficult option for the child of the great artist is to become a Nestbeschmutzer and innovate past the work of their father or in reaction against it, inevitably ensuring that they will suffer the fate of usurping their beloved parent, which will likely haunt them until they are orphaned, or estrange them from their parent forever. I fail to recall any artists who have done this, because, of course, the vast majority of the children of famous artists rarely achieve anything precisely because they are famous artists' children. What Eugene does is clearly the most detestable thing, however, I thought as I sat on the white sofa, because he entices people to enter into his world under the illusion that he is some kind of *real* artist who is *interested in interrogating* things—he actually says this nonsentence, *I am interested in interrogating things*, he says it out loud—and even still people are ensnared by his charm because he's seduced them with his *surroundings*, which screech *intellectual*. They're ensnared by his disingenuous eyeglasses, his disingenuously frayed T-shirt, by his toothy jackal's smile, they're ensnared by him under the apprehension that he is interested in making art and sharing ideas, and they share their ideas with him and then he cannibalizes them for his advertisements. This was part of the reason that I had to break with him and Nicole permanently, I thought, when I left the city without telling them. It was the only way that I could extricate myself from their twisted and sadistic life, which I had become so wrapped up in. When I was living with them in the Bowery, they always knew where I was. Every time I left the house they knew *where I was going* and would often come with me, and for a long time I loved this, because they also brought me everywhere, to meet the artists and writers that I admired. I thought of Eugene and Nicole as magicians, or fairy godmothers, or gods, because they genuinely knew the people that I had read about, and it felt wonderful to be doted on in this way, to be introduced to people by Nicole as a *promising young person*, as her *promising young friend*. I only came to understand how stifling this was when I began publishing small stories and magazine articles and could finally afford my own apartment in Brooklyn, and I was relieved that I could be freed of the ambient tyranny that was inflicted on me by my two rakish benefactors when I had been living in the Bowery, with their marriage that was impossible to refer to as *failing* because they had chosen not to get married as some kind of political gesture, and their *sexual openness* with everyone in their orbit that was supposed to be *enlightened* but made people feel they had to *perform* for them. But even when I was free and was no longer living with them on the Bowery, because I am a terrible weakling who is so desirous of luxury and comfort, I couldn't resist driving with them to their *farmhouse* in Rhine-beck, the beautiful compound up the Hudson River full of art and interesting furniture, for a weekend of relaxation *in nature* surrounded by every creature comfort I had been so cruelly deprived of in my apartment in Brooklyn: a roll-top bathtub stocked with sandalwood scented cosmetic products, fine linens, and most importantly, an extensive library, a library full of literature, back issues of art magazines, and a section that Nicole and Eugene referred to as *theory*, which encompassed literary criticism, philosophy, museum catalogs, psychoanalytic studies, and history monographs, all organized under the term *theory*. They loved *reading theory*, this single monolithic thing called *theory books*, which were in reality unified only by the fact that their spines were universally uncracked, their pages unopened, and their ideas, their *theories*, utterly unknown by their owners. I was incredibly lucky to have this library, because though they did not read, they had wonderful taste in literature, or at least had figured out what to buy from someone with wonderful taste in literature. They had every book that they *should have*, every book that would be excluded from a *classical education* but was so necessary for an education in the arts, the missing pieces for me, and so I loved to sit in the jute bucket chair in the library with the cashmere throw blanket reading until I was summoned for dinner or a walk or whatever activity I had to partake in to earn my keep in the wonderful Rhinebeck house. Sitting in the corner seat of the sofa at Eugene and Nicole's apartment, I realized that I had once again been ensnared by the comfortable and chic furnishings that this couple had habitually trapped me in, after all that I had done to extract myself from their influence I was once again surrounded by their spare sumptuousness, and I watched as the others who had been lured here by Eugene or Nicole or the promise of the actress waited for the honored guest to arrive. These people had more or less all been at Rebecca's funeral earlier that day, and so I watched as each newcomer performed a sort of bizarre ritual with those already at the party, a ritual in which they met each other with a *somber embrace*, they gripped each other by the arms, held each other at arm's length so they could *really see each other*, squeezed each other, and then gave each other a *serious look* to acknowledge that they had *experienced a tragedy together*, and they relished this, because there is no experience more *bonding* than a *shared tragedy*. And then, having both done their duty, they perked up as if *agreeing to put on a brave face*, as if, *for Rebecca*, agreeing to emerge from their sorrow and have a nice time. I actually heard one of the guests—a conceptual artist who always had *flowers in her hair* and who I had always found incredibly stupid and annoying and, last I saw her, five years ago, was always bringing her *baby* to parties and art openings tied to her in an imperfectly dyed cotton sling, and she would tell people that she had brought the baby because indigenous mothers (indigenous to where, she never said) never parted from their babies for the first year, that the increased skin-to-skin contact taught the babies crucial *self-nurturing* skills for later in life, but really I'm not sure that a loft full of cigarette smoke and cocaine-fueled debates about post-internet aesthetics was what the *indigenous mothers* had in mind when they came up with this parenting style—I heard this conceptual artist, for once *sans bébé*, say to Nicole at the door when she'd arrived, *she*

*would have wanted us to have a nice time. She would have wanted us
to celebrate the arts.* It was nice there would be an actor coming
because *she would have wanted us to celebrate drama*, she said to
Nicole, who accepted the conceptual artist's bouquet of white
daffodils and white narcissus flowers, as if she were the one who
was particularly bereaved, Nicole, who said *thank you for these*
with a timbre of sorrow that was so deep yet so *fleeting* that it
vanished from her voice the instant she summoned a caterer to
put the flowers in some water, a sorrow so deep it must have been
hard for her to sustain, and the conceptual artist joined the rest of
the party who *honored the dramatic arts* in their greetings to one
another, their faces like the masks that represent the theater, per-
forming greetings that were at first incredibly grave, deeply
somber, and then, no more than five seconds later, dropping the
solemnity and smiling, beaming even. And I watched these performances from the comfort of my seat on the sofa, I watched as
the silliest people in all of New York, New York, which is of
course *the greatest city on earth*, therefore making these people
the silliest people *in all of the world*, I watched as they exchanged
their condolences for the second time that day, and I made a fist
and hit myself in the upper thigh repeatedly, as I am known to do
in moments of boredom or vexation, I thwacked myself in the
upper thigh, really pounded at myself, and thought *you are an
idiot*, yes, you are *an absolute idiot* for coming here, for dragging
yourself back here, to the place where you once were *desperate* to
be invited. You were once *so desperate* to know these people, you
once *maneuvered* to get to know these people, being in their

company made you feel *so special*, you *loved* these people, and I thwacked myself in the leg again and again with my closed fist as I sat on the corner seat of the sofa, I thwacked my thigh and laughed, I really cackled, I cackled because really it made me sad, sad that I could have been such an idiot to have returned here when I had spent the past five years on a veritable *detox plan* from the life on the Bowery, and now people were looking at me, because of the thwacking, and I noticed them looking at me, I acknowledged their looks, and I did stop pounding at my leg and even so I said hello to no one, and of course though I knew many of the people who entered the room, no one dared to approach me as I have a great talent for standoffishness, for making myself seem as unapproachable and vicious as possible, though of course they are the vicious ones. At that moment I saw that Alexander was sitting across from me in the same model of Bauhaus jute bucket chair that Nicole had in Rhinebeck and became overwhelmed with an even deeper feeling of dread and humiliation at my return to this house and its comforts, at my presence in this palace of tarted-up vapidity. Eugene's meticulously decorated apartment, which had once made me feel like I was in a *place for intellectuals*, now disgusted me. It was the feeling that I was *in a place for intellectuals* that made me feel so ill. That the apartment was constructed as a temple to intellectual activity felt dirty. The perfection of the apartment, and its distressed bubinga wood bench that looked like it had spent several decades at the bottom of the sea after falling off a clipper ship, and its lacquered yellow console that felt futuristic and modern in its garish break with conventional homeware. The effect of the apartment was to stun those who entered. It wasn't just the size, though the loft was so open and vast that it shocked even wealthy people with large apartments, but what really made the apartment stand out was that it was so deliberate, so unique in its design. It was not *eclectic* and *boho-chic*, like the homes of wealthy people who *love to travel*, nor covered with *tapestries* and *African masks* like the homes of psychoanalysts, nor was it *minimalist*, *sterile*, and *cold*, like the homes of so many wealthy art collectors and technocrats. Eugene and Nicole's loft was an idiosyncratic temple to good taste. Their furniture, which was expensive but not gaudy, fit perfectly with their art collection, which was even more expensive but purposefully unrecognizable. It is better, I thought as I sat on the white linen sofa, when your apartment mainly conveys your wealth as it does in the homes of the old wealthy—in which there are Louis XV chairs covered in gold leaf, hand-painted wallpaper, ornate rococo plaster moldings, and ivory commodes made from the tusks of poached African elephants—though in a sense there are also, in those homes, mahogany bookcases with full runs of leather-bound editions, their pages uncut, which make them similar to the brightly colored steel modular shelves here at Eugene's. In fact, I thought, the tasteful and wealthy have done this for all of time, used their furniture to convey the intelligence, the knowledge of the world that naturally accompanies their class, but only recently has this furniture begun to look similar to the slapdash furnishings of the young and the broke. Yes, I thought as I sank deeply into the white sofa, it is the home-furnishing equivalent of those trendy six-hundred-dollar calfskin sneakers that come with holes on the sides, but just like the sneakers, it is crucial that the level of comfort is different, and as I recalled Rebecca's old apartment on Ludlow Street, the hovel with a roommate that shared many aesthetic similarities with the grand apartment on the Bowery—exposed red brick, large bookcases, a mattress directly on the floor—but Rebecca, though she was surrounded by the aesthetic markers of good taste, was deprived the comfort of Eugene and Nicole's apartment, though she could enjoy it a few nights a week when she visited the spare, well-decorated version of her own home for dinner. And just as Eugene cannibalized the artistic innovations of his poorer, more creative friends for profit, sapping their ideas of all their revolutionary potential, so too did his apartment's design capitalize on the aesthetic of his poorer friends' houses, re-creating their things and approximating their surroundings in more lavish materials, the things his friends had painstakingly combed through flea markets for, the things they had purchased precisely because they saw something wonderful, something specific to their tastes, in objects that nobody else cared for. Eugene would come into their homes and remark on the beauty of these things, compliment his friends in the most genuine way on their seashell-covered clock or their mustard-yellow school bench picked off the curb, taking mental notes on their dimensions, their character, and with a carefully honed skill that only the child of an artist with great taste and extra money could possess, he would remake these special items in finer fabrics and slightly more refined shapes, and would later in a sadistic maneuver casually invite his friends to visit and, without drawing attention to it, there would be the new cashmere-and-mohair version of their patterned scratchy wool thrift store blanket, he would pour them a Coca-Cola from the matching set of Murano glass tumblers he'd found at an auction house after seeing their sole, prized cup, used only as a decoration in order to preserve it. The luxury of his re-creations ruined the look of one's own things *for the very people he had stolen them from*, but even worse than this, even more sinister, was the intentional carelessness that Eugene and Nicole had with their expensive and luxurious things, which made one feel absolutely foolish for cherishing one's possessions as if they were precious when they were so worthless in comparison. If Eugene could, without a second thought, rest a hot mug of tea on a mahogany coffee table without reaching for one of his etched marble coasters, then how foolish it was to protect and cherish one's own pine table, how *middle class* it was to protect cheap lacquered pine wood from heat rings when Eugene had such a free spirit, ready to destroy something far more beautiful, ready to turn a luxury object into that shabby-chic lived-in style because he seemingly didn't care at all about his belongings—they were *just objects*, just *things*—while you cared deeply about the preservation of low-quality things and bad furniture that wasn't even worth preserving, because you were a boring materialist idiot. I brushed my hand against the cashmere blanket slung over the arm of the sofa, the blanket that was a facsimile of the one Rebecca had knit for

herself from a scratchy red wide-weave mohair and spread across
the bed of her apartment on Ludlow Street. I remembered one
winter afternoon I took the subway over from my apartment in
Brooklyn to Rebecca's to work on a film script I was helping her
write, a short film for her to direct and star in because she said
this was what she needed to get her *career off the ground*, and
when her roommate, her childhood friend from Massachusetts,
Emily, a terribly kind, overweight, lesbian photographer's assistant, who in fact organized the memorial that all who were gath-
ered tonight at Eugene and Nicole's dinner attended that very
morning, when Emily let me in, I found Rebecca at three o'clock
in the afternoon in bed wrapped in that red blanket wearing an
elegant white nightgown, either fast asleep or mimicking a play-
sleep to demonstrate her artistic temperament to me. Rebecca
was always doing this—collapsing in the street, waking up at
eight p.m., staying awake for seventy-two hours straight—to
demonstrate her artistic temperament. In a sense, however ridiculous it was that having nontraditional sleep cycles was her ten-
uous claim to living an artistic lifestyle, when I saw Rebecca so
committed to her play-sleeping, wrapped in the red blanket,
trembling slightly, it was undeniable that she had both the beauty
and the talent to understand the constituent parts of human behavior required of a great actress. How crass, how unbelievably
crass it was of Eugene to have displayed this blanket here at the
dinner directly following her memorial service in Coney Island.
It was a test, I thought, as I watched Eugene, who appeared even
drunker than I'd remembered him, speaking to a young woman

I did not know and rubbing her leg. The blanket was a test that Eugene had set for the rest of us to see *who really knew Rebecca*, who were her *true friends*, who would recognize her things. The fact that he had elected himself to be the proctor of this test, sure that he was the one who knew Rebecca best, that he was the guardian of her memory, made me laugh to myself in the corner seat of the sofa, laugh hard and shake with laughter until I noticed that the people in the sitting area were all looking at me. I had said hardly anything since I came in and now here I was, laughing heartily by myself, and so naturally everyone was looking at me, except for Eugene, who was busy drunkenly wrapping his arms around the neck and shoulders of this young woman I did not know, the young woman I had been told was an *emerging* artist, whose neck was forced to wear Eugene's arms as a thick hairy scarf, the effect of which was to make her body tense up, forcing her face into one of quiet inward despair, a face that either only I saw or only I could recognize, while Eugene whispered something into her ear and then threw his own free head back laughing. I realized then that Eugene was not using Rebecca's blanket as a test to see who knew her best. Even that cynical gesture would be better than the reality, which was of course that he had completely forgotten about the origin of the blanket, that Rebecca had ever had one that looked the same, that he had ever seen it at her house and had it spun from nicer yarn. To him, from the moment he'd had it copied, any relation to Rebecca was dissolved because when he liked something, suddenly it was his. He and Rebecca were perfectly matched in this regard. If Eugene was fixated on accruing objects that allowed him to appropriately express his personality, to the point of course that he had little time left to actually produce anything beyond the impression that he was an artist, Rebecca was convinced that vacating her *self*, destroying and disavowing anything that could be construed as a *characteristic*, was central to her craft as an actress. She'd learned this acting technique at the prestigious drama school where she'd studied with the best acting faculty in the country alongside actors who are now household names. When she was young, she studied both ballet and acting, with no stated preference for either form. No, what she was drawn to was the imperative to submit completely. To the choreographer, to the script, to the director. What she loved most was vacating her body, inviting in the complete domination of some great authority. She was committed to rejecting anything that could be considered her own agency, to the point that she was always waiting for instruction from those around her. Rebecca was, however, a brilliant person. She was without equal in the art of winning people over to her side, at inviting them to create roles for her, to write entire plays for her to perform in, but her tactic was the same as her acting philosophy: to place herself completely at the mercy of whomever she had asked to create a work for her, but in a manner that flattered the person to whom she was appealing, that touched on their own insecurities. To make herself seem so pathetic and desperate for rescue that you would have to do something to support her, but that you were honored that she believed in you enough to tie herself to your art for support. This was the condition by which we became friends, I realized as I sat on the sofa. I'd met Rebecca through Eugene and Nicole in this very room, I remembered as I sat on the white sofa, around the time that I had first begun living with them on the Bowery. She was invited over for one of their dinner parties like the one I was now waiting to begin, by Alexander, who had told me he was *making a study of her* as background for a story he was writing. I was won over immediately by the way that she managed to make me feel as if I were magnetic and important, by throwing herself at my feet the first opportunity that she had, imploring me to come to her apartment and write something with her, that she could tell I was a wonderful writer from just the few moments we had spent together. *You are an actress?* she had asked me, as I sat in this very corner seat of the sofa years ago. When I told her I was not, she insisted that I was a director. *You have a face full of intuition*, she said. *You move in a way that shows you understand human emotion.* She said that this was why I would prove to be an excellent writer, a famous and talented writer, because I had the *instinct of an actress* and, *without question*, because I had made my way to Eugene and Nicole's and I was *oh so young*, I had the *insight of a writer*. Rebecca had an incredible talent for flattery, for picking targets and for knowing exactly what to say to someone to make them feel understood, indebted to her for her kindness, but also somewhat *guilty*— guilty if you didn't return the compliments, and even guiltier if you didn't ask her to collaborate, because it meant that you did not believe the same things about her. So of course, out of a

mixture of guilt and a gluttonous desire to be around Rebecca
and her compliments longer, I did ask her if she would like to
work together on a script, and during our first meeting in her
apartment on Ludlow she unscrewed a double bottle of Chilean
red wine—not a wine shop magnum, a grocery store double
bottle—and I sat on her bed and learned Rebecca's life story.
She'd been raised in the suburbs of Boston; her Italian-American
mother had grown up in the working-class south end of the city,
and she was sure that her grandfather had been a low-level mafioso, which had accounted for her mother's unremitting nervous-
ness and also her refusal (though she had wanted to join the
Boston social elite) to iron out her *southie* accent because of her
fear of dialectally abandoning Rebecca's grandfather, who they
both adored, and who had always called her mother Legs, because she had the most fabulous legs, said Rebecca. Her father
was an early IT specialist, cold and distant, and perhaps slightly
autistic in the way that many other brilliant Jewish men are, who
made *a killing* setting up the computer networks for the public
school systems of Massachusetts before losing the Cape house in
the divorce to her mother and then subsequently most of his
money in the dot-com bubble burst. Soon Rebecca felt a new-
found unease at her school, where she had been at the top of the
class and once among the wealthiest students, ashamed to realize
at the age of ten that the bracelet her mother gave her was more
expensive than the price on a *for sale* sign on a car in her grandparents' neighborhood. She had been notorious at school, she
had told me as we sat on the bed in her terrible apartment on

Ludlow, for her expensive clothing and outré fashion sense, and when her father had lost his money she had started stealing dresses and boots from expensive boutiques on Newbury Street so that her friends wouldn't notice the change in her financial situation. The earliest acting performances she could remember were her casual strolls with perfect ballet posture out the front door of these Boston boutiques, and also of course the great performances she put into the management of the fractious relationship between her father and mother, which required teenaged Rebecca to alternate between playing, every second weekend, for her father, the sweet and studious *Becca* who *had never even wanted a car* for her sixteenth birthday, to soothe his conscience about his financial imprudence in the modest Boston apartment he shared with his *tennis doubles partner*, and then, for the remainder of her time, to perform for her beautiful mother the *Rebecca*, here she stressed the *Re*, that she would eventually settle into more permanently, to embody, in her mother's overly grand, impossible-to-maintain summer home—lived in all year round along with three terribly behaved cockapoos—the glamorous, well-bred, alluring version of herself who had been brought up for want of nothing and would go on to live the happy and exciting life that was of utmost importance to her mother, she would cash in on the check that was the family legs, as her mother cooked multicourse Italian dinners that were far too rich and abundant for the two thin women. Rebecca told me all of this during our first meeting in her apartment on Ludlow Street, picking apart her life with a vulnerability that felt genuine but also over-rehearsed, as if she had been telling this story about herself for so long that she had mastered being overcome by sadness, timed the pained breaks in her voice as part of her repertoire, in the same way that you see the Hare Krishna chanters by Tompkins Square Park having ecstatic visions with such frequency that you wonder if their monumental display of body-shaking transcendence feels a whole lot more like a sneeze. Rebecca had been accepted to a prestigious liberal arts college in Massachusetts and to a famous acting school in New York and had chosen the latter, not only to escape New England and her parents, but also because, she said, *it went without question that I was the smartest person in most rooms*, she said, she took her academic achievement for granted, *what mattered to me*, she said, *and to my mother was that I was the most beautiful woman in a room.* The acceptance to the most prestigious acting school for Hollywood actors proved that she was beautiful. And she *was* beautiful. She had long black hair and big brown eyes, deeply set but still almost bulging out of her pale face, bow-shaped lips over which a lightly visible mustache hovered. I had once told her, I recalled as I sat on the white sofa, that she had an Elvira, Mistress of the Dark–like quality, which had hurt her feelings because Elvira was a *sideshow* and Rebecca had wanted to be a *serious actress*. But she would say things that were intended to make herself seem *dark*, like when she put on a black satin negligee and said *this belonged to a girl who had a party in the West Village and then the boy I'm dating stole it from her and then she died and now it's mine*, and she paused to look at herself in the mirror and then said *it's cool, right?* Over the course of two weeks, together in her bedroom, we drank a kiddie pool's worth of cheap double bottles and she smoked about a million Camels lying in bed rattling off stories about herself, about her deep feelings of loneliness, about a childhood spent acting for both of her parents, about her dual quests to obliterate herself and to search desperately for something she could call a *self.* Meanwhile I sat at the foot of the bed with a tape recorder and a yellow legal pad taking minutes for what would eventually become the short film we made together about her childhood, *Child Star*, which we filmed in her mother's house in Cape Cod. It was mostly set in her bedroom, unchanged since she was a teenager, the walls painted purple and covered in posters of movie stars, not even obscure movie stars, but the most obvious movie stars that one could think of. The more obvious they were, the more she idolized them. She had the classic photo of Audrey Hepburn in *Breakfast at Tiffany's*, with a cigarette holder and wearing the tiara, framed next to the photo of Marilyn Monroe's skirt billowing up over a subway grate. In a sense it was a joke to her, the way she idolized these actresses, but part of Rebecca's affect was that she loved the most mainstream things. She made no posture toward loving the obscure, and she knew that by identifying ardently and publicly with the tacky, the hackneyed, and the obvious, she was making a deadpan joke about her own unrelenting desire for the fame and popular acceptance that she had yet to attain, even though she knew that most of her friends would likely find this careerism vulgar. This was the subject of our

film: her desire for fame. It played at a small festival and got
some decent press in one major newspaper and got Rebecca tremendously excited about her prospects as an actress, it lifted her
from a depression that she had been suffering from before I knew
her, a depression that had begun on her twenty-sixth birthday,
when she had started to feel like she was becoming too old for
her career to take off and that perhaps it was time for her to *throw
in the towel*. It made me feel happy that I could play a role in her
happiness, that she could admit to people she was actually thirty,
that her introduction of *I'm an actress* no longer carried the ad-
dendum *technically*. She really *was* an actress. The film also
helped me to secure what I then thought were jammy sinecures
writing for fashion magazines, jobs that I had yet to discover
would cost me the price of my soul. Whenever there is money to
be easily made one forgets to account for the price in net losses of
soul. You must remember that the price of every *salade niçoise*
expensed to a fashion magazine is paid for in *soul*, and that after
you've asked enough *emerging artists* about their *morning routine*,
the things they *cannot live without*, items that they *can't live without*, the things that they *cannot live without*, you begin to wonder
where on earth your soul has escaped to, until you track it down
to the Condé Nast ePayables invoicing site. Rebecca's soul was
also slowly attenuated, diminished largely because of her failure
to actually land any of the parts she tried to embody for weeks
only to lead to an unsuccessful audition, and so she would go up
to her mother's house in Cape Cod to recover. I would frequently
go up to visit her there, I thought as I sat on the sofa, in the house

Rebecca had died in, to work together on more film ideas, to relax in the spaciousness of the house and to breathe the soothing sea air. It was jarring to see Rebecca so at home in the country, having imagined her to be a native Bostonian, a product, like me, of the city, unfamiliar with nature, afraid of a horizon uninterrupted by tall buildings. But Rebecca had really grown up in the country, I realized, when I went to her mother's house on the Cape, a house where the neighbors were out of sight, and the windows overlooked only a path lined with beach plums and rose hips that led to the sea. It made Rebecca's narrative that she had grown up *precariously* seem hilarious when I thought of my childhood bedroom, which could comfortably fit only my bed, which touched the wall on three sides, and a small chest of drawers, the price of living in a normal apartment in New York. In the guest room at Rebecca's mother's house, I even had my own en suite bathroom, where I would take long baths after Rebecca and I trudged through the creek that, at low tide, emptied itself of water and became a muddy trail that we walked along in old sneakers Rebecca kept for just this purpose. We would look down at the mud, hunting on the surface for the little air bubbles that Rebecca taught me meant mussels and clams lurked below, and I was amazed that my friend Rebecca, this thirty-year-old woman who was genuinely the most glamorous person I had ever met, knew how to do this, that even with her black eyeliner on, she would dig up the clams and bring them back to her mother by the basketful—that she would wash them and make us spaghetti alle vongole and it was fantastic to eat food that we had found ourselves. It had never even crossed my mind that I could find food myself, especially clams, which cost twenty-six dollars a bag at the markets in the city, for free, and I felt like Rebecca and her mother were geniuses for their self-sufficient luxury. We would give some of the uglier clams to her mother's dogs, who had free run of the place and would yip unendingly throughout the day until Rebecca's mother turned on the television and played films that featured other dogs, the only thing that would quiet them. I loved Rebecca's mother, who I would spend hours alone with while Rebecca slept late into the afternoon. Either because she liked me or because she didn't have anyone else to talk to, she told me the story of her life, the story of her childhood in a rough Boston neighborhood where, though it was full of violence, she was never harmed. She was proud of the fact that she was never harmed. She smiled when she said *no one would ever touch me*, because she was thinking of her family's protecting force, the power that her mafioso father had in the neighborhood, and the physical power of her older brothers, who were tall and handsome and strong and likely also engaged in petty crime. Nothing violent, she said, but because of her brothers, though she grew up in a dangerous place she was never hurt, but because of this neighborhood she had been forced to develop a tougher exterior than her daughter, her daughter who she often worried about because she had been raised without anything to fear, her daughter who as a child had once given a fifty-dollar bill to a man who said he needed help buying a train ticket, an obvious scam—and she was in a sense proud of her daughter's naïveté, because it meant that she had been raised with no reason to distrust the world, but it also made her feel incredibly *alienated* from her. It made her feel like her daughter was the kind of person who could not survive the childhood that *she'd had herself*, that her own daughter might have been afraid of her if they'd been young together, which she often felt when she couldn't contain her anger and screamed at Rebecca, something she tried never to do but occasionally she had to express her feelings the only way she knew how, and actually she thought it was important to be passionate occasionally, that the violence of her childhood and the feeling of protection in the face of danger felt better in a lot of ways than the bland security that came with her *moving up in the world*, she said, gesturing at the neutral-toned kitchen and tapping her manicured nails on the marble countertop, where she was protected from the animal urges of humanity but cut off from the passion and vibrancy of that world. Really, she said, she had always preferred a genuine slap in the face to the ways that more *civilized* people like Rebecca's father fuck you over. But, she had said, her primary goal was to make sure her daughter grew up without the fear of violence that had conditioned her own teenage years, and so one morning she thanked me while Rebecca was still asleep for being Rebecca's friend, for taking care of her and protecting her and for never taking advantage of her, because the daughter wasn't as tough as the mother due to the softness of her upbringing, and her mother cautioned me that Rebecca had an overly trusting nature, which she thanked me again for never taking advantage of and for

protecting her from people who would, because she could tell I
was tough, which had the effect of making me feel as though I
*had* taken advantage of Rebecca although I had never considered
our relationship in those terms, what *advantage* Rebecca could
bring me. To me, our relationship had been one of artistic discovery. Rebecca's room was my schoolhouse, a place where I
could learn from this older, beautiful, glamorous woman who
was surrounded by people at every gallery opening, who was the
center of every party, who wanted to spend time with me and my
ideas, and I was believed in, my ideas were nurtured but also
criticized by someone who had truly a great understanding of art
and film without *holding it over you*. While I lived with Eugene
and Nicole, it was almost as if Rebecca's apartment on Ludlow
was my studio and my refuge. The idea that I could take advantage of Rebecca had never crossed my mind because I cherished
her friendship so deeply, and because she was such a huge force
to me that I didn't then understand how easily she could be dominated, which, I thought as I sat on the white sofa, was either
genuine naïveté because I was almost ten years younger than
her, or really, I thought, it was more likely willful ignorance.
When her mother said this to me in her navy velour sweatpants,
I understood that Rebecca had inherited her mother's unusual
combination of anxiety and toughness. I watched the way her
mother would cower with fear when the dogs barked and then
suddenly toughen up, steeling herself, making tight little fists
and berating them in her hoarse Bostonian, and then change
course again to smooth her forehead and dole out lavish dog

treats, rewarding their bad behavior. Rebecca had inherited her mother's long legs and erratic histrionics and good hospitality, hospitality that Eugene and Nicole knew nothing about, I thought as I sat on the sofa, becoming increasingly drunk on an empty stomach, as the night crept past what the world knows as dinnertime and into a period only the Spanish would consider suitable for eating, because, as Nicole announced, we were *waiting for the actress*, whose premiere was *running long*. Rebecca was an excellent cook, although when it was only the two of us working together we rarely ate much. There was a period when she had a serious boyfriend, a handsome six-foot-five-inch former mid-ranking chess master who grew up on the Lower East Side and had given up playing competitively when he was a teenager because of nerves and now taught private-school children the Ruy Lopez and the Sicilian Defense. She became slavishly devoted to the Chess Player, who would sit and lift weights in her apartment, only working on his arms so that the rest of his body looked freakishly mangled and thin when taken in with his enormous biceps that were always engaged in computer chess. Emily, who Rebecca still lived with then, more or less moved upstate with the photographer she worked for during this period, about two years all in. Emily said she had to be up there for weeks at a time because the photographer needed help looking after her daughters, but it seemed she was just too polite and submissive to Rebecca to mention her boyfriend's unending presence was *invading her space*. He called their place the *skittles room* because that's where noncompetitive chess games are played at tournaments, but that aside, from what I understood, he was a smart guy. He was possessive of Rebecca, so she said, and for a period of months during the relationship no one saw her at all because it made him jealous when she went places without him. He didn't like other people so he never went out, and so neither did she. Rebecca channeled the energy she had once reserved for acting and socializing into cooking complex Italian dinners, playing the role of a housewife in a bad movie set in the 1950s, but she never complained about this when I saw her for the occasional walk around the neighborhood—this was the only way I could see her because the chess master was apparently *afraid of my influence*, which in a sense flattered me, so we would go on walks around the neighborhood, usually stopping into Di Palo's for sausages for their dinner, and then we'd walk to the expensive wine store and I would give my opinion on a wine pairing, because Rebecca didn't really drink if she didn't have to, she mostly abused prescription painkillers, and because Nicole had taught me how to select wines after I once brought a red she said was undrinkable up to Rhinebeck. It was almost as if Rebecca playing the dutiful housewife was the most content I'd ever seen her. She immersed herself totally into this role, and I thought it gave her some kind of sense of order—the same feeling of ease she felt while she was acting, that she was meant to be listening to the director, that she was meant to be vacating her *self*. I didn't hear much from Rebecca during the years that she spent in the *skittles room*. I had ceased to live with Eugene and Nicole during that time, but I still went to their house almost every night for dinner, and I had become much closer with Alexander, who was also barred from the *skittles room*, though he had been closest to Rebecca, I thought as I sat on the corner seat of the sofa, looking at Alexander in his Prince of Wales brown tweed suit talking about his latest *literary experiment*. Yes, Alexander had, until my friendship with Rebecca, been closest to her and had introduced me to her, and even *he* had been barred from the *skittles room*, which had actually made me jealous in a way, that the chess master thought *Alexander was a threat* to her attention as much as I was, which made me wonder at the time about the nature of Alexander and Rebecca's relationship. I remember that I was always anxious to hear about what was going on with Rebecca during this period, not only because I missed our afternoons together, I missed her as a collaborator, but because I had this secret hope that aside from making lasagna she was secretly working on something great and her face would suddenly pop up in a newspaper, her name on a marquee or on one of those advertising pyramids on top of taxicabs. I hoped that she had something in the works that would lead to her *name in flashing lights*, and it struck me as a great pity that Rebecca was as yet unable to transform her great talent for capturing human emotion into the theatrical stardom that she so desperately craved. And then I heard from Nicole, one of the few members of our little crew that she remained in close contact with, that during this period Rebecca was able to secure for herself a sort of residency at a small theater downtown, that she had financial backing from a producer who had taken an interest in her and had given her a space

in his theater to perform whatever she wanted. Nicole went to
see the performance, and she asked me, just afterward, years
ago, as I sat in the same seat on the sofa that I sat in now, if I had
heard about Rebecca's show, and I said *yes*, lying, I said, *yes, I
heard it was great*, to which Nicole replied, *who on earth told you
that?* And then we both laughed for a long time. It clearly brought
Nicole great pleasure to inform me that Rebecca's artistic endeavor was useless, that, as Nicole had wished for everyone in
her orbit, Rebecca amounted to little more than a person Nicole
brought around to parties, and that Nicole could demonstrate to
me, her protégé, her *protectee*, that she would always be more
powerful and more useful as a friend than Rebecca, that I had
been foolish for even thinking that I might migrate my life's center of gravity from Nicole to Rebecca, which made me feel embarrassed because I had picked up on that thought of Nicole's
only because I realized she was right. Nicole said the show had
been a total disaster. Rebecca had delivered a monologue about
her life, about her childhood, that was *in equal parts incoherent
and tragic*. This was why, I thought, listening to Nicole, Rebecca
needed other people to write her material for her. All those years
I'd listened to Rebecca talk about herself, about her childhood,
and I never thought she really understood herself, I always believed she needed someone, whether it was me or someone else,
to tell her *who she was*, to be confessional *for her to her* because her
entire identity was in constant flux. I always believed that Rebecca had no idea who she was, I could see that her own stories
about herself did not align, so naturally writing a monologue

about her life, a life story that was so mixed up in her head, was impossible without the guidance of some other cowriter or, actually, even better, a therapist. Although Rebecca was clever and charming she never could tell a coherent story, because what interested her more than story was artifice and spectacle, artifice and pageantry, which works for a performance of the Rockettes but not as well for a confessional one-woman show that is married to literal depictions of a woman's life. This is what I'd thought about my dear friend Rebecca, and in fact, Nicole said, in the performance Rebecca often referenced things that her therapist had said about her childhood, often referenced the frameworks that her therapist had given her to think about her childhood. She would say *my therapist says I think this because . . .* as if she needed the external analytical authority for her *own thoughts* about *her own life* to be meaningful. Though she was not interested in the postmodern, according to Nicole she did make her audience suffer so much that in a sense the show was as postmodern as Perec. She said the whole performance felt like when Rebecca got too drunk at a party and trapped someone who was enticed by her—or enticed by the seemingly important place she had in the *artistic world*—forcing them to listen to her half-truths about her childhood and quarter- or eighth-truths about her romantic life, which when it happened was entertaining if a bit sad, but, unlike the show, when Rebecca trapped you in the corner at a party it did not last for over an hour and it was free. Nicole didn't actually admit to the idea that people had attended the performance because they were enticed by Rebecca's place in the

artistic world, because it would have wounded her to admit that
Rebecca had any great draw for people aside from being a set
piece of her dinner parties, but the rest of what she said about the
show made me feel like I had to ignore the Chess Player's fatwa
and see the performance for myself. I considered buying a ticket
from a friend of Nicole's who couldn't make the performance but
I was worried that this would get back to Rebecca, who I remember feeling so annoyed by, so hurt by, really, that I didn't
even want to give her the power of reading my name written
down, even looking at the letters that spelled my name, especially in relation to her own name. So on one of what would be
the final nights of the show I went to the box office a few hours
early, careful to time this with an imagined schedule I had for
Rebecca to avoid a run-in, making sure I'd come after she had
arrived at the theater but before she started peering out the stage
door to watch people filter into the theater. I bought a ticket in
cash and stood in the back, behind the seats, and within the first
fifteen minutes I understood that Nicole meant that Rebecca's
show just was the exact same self-mythologizing, faux-vulnerable
confessional act about her *madness* about her *troubled past* that
she had always put on with people that she didn't know well—
people who she intended to win over, people who she wanted to
protect her—except by literally producing a show of this kind,
by putting the show on a stage with cues for lights and music,
with written-out lines and preplanned moments in which she addressed the audience as friends, she was admitting that the entire
construction of herself that she had been peddling up to that

point was *an act*. By putting on her *persona* as an *act* she was admitting to the fact that even though she told *everyone everything* she really revealed *nothing to anybody*, that even though she was *pouring out her soul* this outpouring was as ritualistic for her as it was for other people to chitchat idly about the prospect of rain, and that whatever it was that she was so desperate to actually hide would *never really come out*. So her show had not been a success. The audience was able to pick up on the fact that this girl, this charming and charismatic girl who was confessing to these *shameful thoughts* was doing it night after night in front of many different audiences, and that the *shameful thoughts* were presented without narrative structure or dramatic tension but as is, and that the *shameful thoughts* she was confessing to, for a society inured to reality television and routine acts of violence, were rather blasé. And so the show closed after only a few performances, once Rebecca ran out of people she knew, or people who had encountered her *in the downtown scene* and wanted to get to know her better, many of them people for whom she had performed much of her *show* at some point in the corner of the room at a party. It made me sad when Nicole told me about the show's closing, Nicole, who thought that I would have relished the opportunity to hear that Rebecca was doing badly because she and I were not in contact. But it only depressed me. It made me feel that I should have demanded Rebecca show me what she was going to perform beforehand, that she allow me to help her organize her thoughts into something more coherent, or maybe even something more honest and more like the film we'd made together. But I knew that it wasn't the lack of my input that made Rebecca's show like this. It wasn't that she needed help from me, or help from anyone. I was of the opinion that Rebecca secretly knew that the show wasn't good, that she was too smart to produce something that was bad without knowing that it was bad, and that she had put on a bad performance on purpose because she didn't genuinely believe in her ability to do anything well, so she didn't try to do it well. It wasn't because she was untalented—quite the contrary. In the same way she couldn't decide if she had grown up in a rarefied environment or if she was a Dickensian heroine born in the workhouse, Rebecca was unable to make her mind up about whether she was a comedic actress or a great dramatist, if she was a writer or a performer, if she really did desire the total submission she constantly sought out, or if she was secretly interested in complete control. She wanted to be both, she wanted to be everything all at once, as she told me when she said that she related most to Esther in *The Bell Jar*, that she *was* Esther in *The Bell Jar*, spending so long trying to pick between the opportunities handed to her on a platter, between her many talents, that because of her excess of talent, her beauty in conflict with her intelligence, her charisma in conflict with her desire to *lock herself away and become a genius*, because of these *contradictions in her character* she couldn't happily devote herself to anything, and because of her paralysis in decision-making she failed at everything. Of course the whole point of *The Bell Jar* is that only through paralysis, through not picking a path, do we exclude the possibility of all paths, and really, I always thought, reading *The*

*Bell Jar* I could sense that Sylvia herself had realized that she was lucky, or that this problem didn't apply to her because the only way to avoid Esther's impossible choice was to write. In writing you could be a dabbler without guilt, you could become interested in medicine for a few months, spend a few years learning about flowers, about shoes, about horses. Your only constant was that you always wrote about it, but you had access to every path and abandoned each one when you tired of it. Why couldn't Rebecca have thought of acting this way, I thought from my seat on the sofa, why couldn't she think of her show as a vehicle to perform every role that she was precluded from living? Why, I thought from my seat on the sofa, was she instead so obsessed with the idea that before she became a *name* she had to decide everything, so she needed to forestall attempting anything that would *make a name for herself* until she decided who that *self* was going to be? This reticence to declare who she was meant that her show had to be this exactly perfect announcement of a static idea of *Rebecca*, like that photo, no, like that death mask of Marilyn Monroe smiling as her dress flies up around her. This is an icon, not a human being, this is who we remember. How *did* I remember Rebecca, I thought as I sat on the corner seat of the sofa. I knew the role she'd played when I'd last seen her, when, after two years together, the chess master eventually left her for his ex-girlfriend, a rich girl who unlike Rebecca had retained her money, and Rebecca called me and I came over from my new apartment next to the Eldridge Street Synagogue, above an all-night internet café slash *massage parlor*, and watched as Rebecca performed the role of distraught, hysterical woman who has realized her life is a lie. When I arrived, she had two televisions, one with a shattered screen, playing *Texas Chainsaw Massacre* in her room at the same time. Her black eyeliner was smeared across her face from crying and she was wearing a short gray satin nightgown lined with black lace. She had naturally thin eyebrows but I still suspected that she had made herself up to look as much like tragedy-era Marlene Dietrich as possible, having told me once about the famous disarray of Dietrich's penthouse apartment for which Hemingway had bought a dining table because he was *tired of eating off of boxes*. Rebecca's own apartment was in a complete state of disarray at all times, but now it was perfectly set designed. There were orange pill bottles on the floor and a bottle of Macallan next to the bed, which she said she'd been having small sips of every hour and asked me if this *made her an alcoholic*. I spent a few hours with her as audience to her histrionics, watching as she stomped around the apartment trailed by a diaphanous negligee, and followed her as she went out into the street half-naked, wearing only the tiny silk thing and low-slung too-big sweatpants, to pick up her tranquilizers, allowing myself to be amused by her display at the Duane Reade, where she screamed *I'm a crazy person* at the pharmacist in a way that really was quite crazy, quite violent. *I am a crazy person*, she screamed, locking eyes with her and laughing hard in the direction of the plexiglass that separated them, though the pharmacist was completely unfazed. In fact the pharmacist was really the best scene partner that Rebecca could ask for, a Lower East Side pharmacist who had evidently seen much worse than a pale bony maniac in a silk negligee with her breasts half-exposed. She was totally unmoved by Rebecca's desperate plea for attention, and in a sense, so was I, even as we returned to her apartment with the pleasingly heavy paper sackful of pills and even as she shook and shouted, *how do I know that I exist, how can I be sure that I exist, who is Rebecca, Rebecca, who is Rebecca,* and even as she repeatedly asked me if I thought she was going crazy. I did not think that she was really going crazy, but I did find the repetitive questions tiresome. I knew she was being intentionally tiresome as a sort of endurance game, to see if anyone could stand her behavior long enough to be with her. If she could act this foolishly, this terribly, and anyone would stay with her, if anyone could stand her worst behavior, it would mean they loved her as the *chess master* could not. So even though outside of her show I hadn't seen her for over a year, she was testing my love for her by trying to see how far she could push me, if I would stay, because she knew I had once loved her more than the Chess Player had. But in the end, when she refused to take the tranquilizer, and instead took tiny little sips from the whiskey bottle by her bed, sips that couldn't get a child drunk and were meant to play a part in her *downtrodden woman routine,* I told her I was leaving and she shouted that I was a *manipulative bitch* and I had *used* her and then *dropped her when I didn't need her anymore,* that I had used her and *abandoned her when I didn't care about her anymore.* So I left her in her little room. I stood up and I left Rebecca's little room and walked down the stairs and I never returned there again. I made my grand exit from her life, and, soon after, I moved to London, and I thought about her less and less, as one does with a friend who falls out of touch, until I forgot about her outright, and I heard nothing from her, or even really about her, until her mother called me to tell me that she was dead. A friend can be the most cherished person in the world to us, I thought as I sat on the corner seat of the sofa, they can open all kinds of worlds to us, we orient our lives around them, we feel as though they are part of our essence, when something new happens to us, we feel the experience is not yet whole until we've told this friend all about it, until we've lived it twice with this cherished friend, this friend who knows so much about us that they cease to become another person and are instead an extension of us. Then suddenly one day they cease to exist in our minds, they cease to be of any importance at all, this friend who we at one point narrated our lives to, discussed every shoe purchase with, who knew what kind of moisturizer we bought, what snack we liked to steal from Whole Foods to have in the movie theater, this friend is completely gone. It is terrifying, the thought that those who were once the absolute center of our lives could disappear so quickly and so permanently from our universe, I thought as I sat on the sofa on the Bowery, it made me feel that even what one perceives to be life's constants—the rats underneath the subway platform, the yellow square of cheese on a tuna melt, Rebecca at Eugene's—can disappear. Rebecca should have been here in this room at Eugene's, exercising her total domination of the guests through her elegance, her charm, her carefully concocted vulnerability, and her ability to actually listen to what people had to say, but the whole Rebecca, as shocking as it was, the whole Rebecca could disappear. Well, she would have loved, I thought as I sat in the corner of the sofa, the way that she disappeared into thin air earlier that day at her memorial, where, I realized, smiling, she was both the director and the star. She would have loved the way her friends, the best of New York's artistic world, fifty or so people, most of whom bitterly hated one another, were forced by the occasion of her death to gather together on the rocks of the Brooklyn winter beach, that they had all appropriately selected their extravagantly dour costumes, Nicole's black leather pants and 1990s Belgian military-style jacket, Alexander surrounded by Eugene and his retinue of young people, to one of whom I heard Nicole say *I'm wearing black for Rebecca, though it's totally out of my character, because she loved black, Rebecca always wore black*, as if everyone at the funeral weren't wearing black, as if it were *unusual* to wear black to a funeral. The whole scene was perfect. The snow fell on Alexander's ghoulish thrift store overcoat that I was glad to see he still wore to emphasize his *disinterestedness in material things*. Was it oversized, or was it just too big for him? Alexander insisted on reading one of his own poems, a long one that he read slowly, pausing at times to look at his feet and touch his heart as if he were battling an uncontrollable swell of emotion, then suddenly finding the *strength* to push ahead, resolutely, like the valiant orator he is, who has found it within himself to carry on, nobly continuing the poem about *supernovae* and *black holes*, in order to finish the recitation that no one had asked for, his long poem that he continually had to pause in order to break down, though he did not cry, to show that he was the greatest friend Rebecca had. When Alexander finished his *meditations on Rebecca*, which had actually included a number of references to how *Rebecca inspired his work*—and he listed the names of plays that had been inspired by her, and also the title of his own novel, a novel that had nothing to do with Rebecca in the slightest—after he had finished with this offensive recitation of his CV, I noticed that a crowd of onlookers, brightly parkaed individuals and even some people in exercise clothes who had paused their runs, had assembled at the edge of the concrete boardwalk at just the moment when Rebecca was to make her grand entrance. Emily withdrew a gallon-sized ziplock bag full of Rebecca's ashes and people began to pass it around, and our star, our director, instructed the mourners, without uttering a command, to reach into the gallon-sized ziplock bag full of her ashes and fling bits of herself into the wind, Rebecca making her grand entrance and at once her great exit, her ashes floating, riding the wind, and dispersing across the snow-covered sand, the only disturbance of the blanket of white aside from the seagull tracks. It was her greatest performance, I thought as I sat on the sofa. Her purest experience of complete submission, which was essentially her domination. For the first time since the previous morning when I had run into Eugene, I felt sick with sadness. Rebecca would have loved to have been there. She would have loved to have been there, I thought as I sat on the sofa and finished my glass of wine. I felt lightheaded and hungry and I heard Nicole conspiring with a film producer whose name I was constantly trying to forget, but then realized I actually had forgotten his name, which greatly amused me and lightly perturbed me. Nicole announced once again that the actress would only be another thirty minutes or so and I felt suddenly enraged. Not because our dinner was delayed by the actress, but because Nicole and Eugene had allowed this dinner's shape and form to be dictated by the actress, this dinner *the night of Rebecca's memorial*, a memorial we had all attended together earlier that day. Each and every person at the dinner had been at Rebecca's memorial that day. And yet this was not a dinner in her honor. We all had to sit in this room, not remembering Rebecca but anticipating the arrival of this actress. But of course, *how could* the dinner be in Rebecca's honor? She hadn't acted in anything in years, and Eugene and Nicole would never give a dinner in honor of someone who hadn't had a big success lately. The unsuccessful could attend, they could bear witness to Eugene and Nicole's attempt to make connections with successful people, but a dinner would not be thrown in their honor. Eugene and Nicole wouldn't throw a dinner *because of Rebecca*, not even for a birthday party, not even for a *wake*! This had always been the case at their loft on the Bowery. Though the *nameless* were always the greatest entertainment, the reason that their apartment became a social hub, they were not the real *draw* of the evenings. The draw was the *famous*, who tended to disappoint because of the practiced tact and discretion that fame requires. I realized, as I sat on the sofa, that my biggest mistake was that I

had come to Eugene and Nicole's after the funeral because I had
wanted to be around Rebecca's close friends, friends who had
known her, who we'd been with together, but this was a failure
of logic: it was like longing to be with the dungeon master because he best understood your torture chamber. Across the
room, Eugene was showing the young artist I didn't recognize a
new piece of art he had bought, and I could hear him say *would
you just loooook at that gesture* with a gleeful tone that made me
smile. There was something hysterically funny about *the multidisciplinary artist* Eugene that even he understood about himself,
something deliciously camp about his behavior, something that
screamed to you from his polka-dotted socks, his round tortoise-
shell spectacles, that made him seem to be the kind of person
who *lived breathed and devoured* art, which was magnetic when
you were close with him even if you knew his campiness and his
love of art was a trompe l'oeil patina painted with shit onto the
sparkling bronze bust that was his inner idiocy, his enduring alcoholism, and, from the way he refused to relinquish the young
artist's elbow, his enduring sex-pestiness. It was pathetic that I
had allowed people as stupid and crass as Eugene and Nicole to
dominate me for so long. I remember a time when we all went to
see Nicole's half brother, a mathematician, defend his thesis at
Columbia and Eugene insisted to me and Nicole in a whisper that
their work was exactly the same, *why hadn't Nicole said their work
was exactly the same*, they both interrogated notions of performa-
tivity, of objects' existence in space, of ontology. Nicole, whose
grandfather left, or rather was banned from, a math

professorship in Austria before coming to America to re-create their family fortune as a banker, understood how much she did not understand about mathematics. So when Eugene raised his hand in the small seminar room as four leading topologists were examining her brother, she began pleading with her *partner* to put it down, pleading with him desperately not to ask a question, holding his yellow-and-orange mohair-ensconced arm and jostling at it, trying to pin it to the wooden bench between them with all her might, unsuccessfully, as Eugene shook her away and stood up, and Nicole's brother, a tall, nervous young man in a rumpled oxford shirt seated across the room, called on his brother-in-law in the middle of his thesis defense by saying *yes, Eugene*. He said *yes, Eugene*, with such a beleaguered and defeated voice, as though he knew it was impossible for him to escape from his sister's partner's humiliation, that it was incredibly difficult to keep my composure, I recalled as I sat in the corner seat of the sofa, attempting to repress the same smile that erupted then over my face. Eugene, in one of the saddest moments I can remember, said only *this was a fantastic presentation*, which shocked me, and was in a sense worse than if he had humiliated himself publicly. It was a great letdown that he didn't ask his question, I thought. It ruined the purpose of Eugene in my eyes. He had moderated himself and therefore he had humiliated himself, and now, as I sat in the corner of the white sofa, I realized that was the last time I had seen Eugene before encountering him on the Bowery. I had been so disgusted with his cowardice, that he believed he truly did understand everything in the mathematics lecture but was too afraid to speak in front of the mathematicians, and it was this lack of self-confidence that made me feel I could finally cut ties with Eugene and Nicole once and for all, I thought as I sat on the sofa, now drinking a glass of orange wine from Georgia, this total humiliation of Eugene as he sputtered out the request for Nicole's brother to repeat himself and cowered back, defeated, into his place on the bench. A few days after the presentation I ignored Eugene's invitation to accompany him to some gallery dinner, and then some phone calls from Nicole, and eventually I had managed to avoid them almost completely, save some close shaves at openings, for a year or two until I left New York for Rome to work on a film script with a Roman film director that never saw the light of day, and in Rome, at last free of the little set on the Bowery, I met people, or not people, rather, I should say aristocrats, who are not human, really, and should not be referred to as such, in the director's acquaintance who rivaled or even surpassed Eugene's profligate and licentious behavior. This further lowered Eugene in my estimation, because if you're going to be a terrible person, at least be the most terrible, the crassest, the evilest, I thought as I sat on my seat on the sofa, having found myself sat in the same seat I had occupied at dinner parties for years before fleeing from this house on the Bowery and vowing never to return. Eugene had taken advantage of my fragile emotional state when he saw me outside of that café. He must have known that I was in shock about the death of Rebecca, and he'd used that information to ambush me, he may have followed me for all I know. He may have seen me get off the subway and then planted himself in the window seat of the café, knowing I'd pass it, so that he could emerge like Grendel's mother, that monster, from his health food restaurant cave and attack me when my guard was down. He must have known that I was well aware of Rebecca's death, that I was distraught and vulnerable, and used this to sneak up on me and drag me back to the loft on the Bowery, he must have known that he would use the excuse of honoring the actress to further disorient me, and that he could easily prey upon my weakness— the weakness that he knew so well from the years during which I lived with him. He never ceased to take advantage of my capitulatory character. He knew that I would easily capitulate to agree to watch whatever middlebrow contemporary French cinema he wanted, capitulate to agreeing with his political ideas, capitulate to his sexual advances. I should have known that I was always, from the moment the plane touched down at Kennedy two months ago, that I was always going to capitulate to Eugene's invitation, that there would be an invitation from Eugene and Nicole to return to the Bowery and that I would capitulate to it because there is some kind of preening obsequiousness in my character, there has always been a kind of pathetic smarm about me, a babyish smarm that comes from a creeping suspicion that should I lose the people that love me now, I will never again find a single friend on this earth. I think this even as I have made a life for myself in London, a nice life full of more or less intelligent people who, though they are artists, journalists, writers, though they write films and are often successful, unlike the people that crowd around the loft in the Bowery they do not update you, I thought as I overheard Alexander doing at that very moment, as I sat on the white sofa, they do not update you on the meetings they had with their agent about the potential for the rights for their novel to be purchased by a major film studio, they do not pass their phones back and forth to show each other emails from movie producers under the guise of asking other guests at the dinner party to help *decode the email* in an effort to prove to one another that they are serious operators, literally, as Eugene has done, *shown people work emails at dinner*, pretending that they made him feel silly and asking for advice, when really he was just trying to name-drop someone that I had often never even heard of. In fact, some may say that the English are incredibly reserved and that this is the reason that it's rare to hear them discussing the names of their agents, the meetings that they're taking, but in reality it is that they are rightfully ashamed of caring about these things. They do not hide them once they are pressed to discuss the practicalities of their careers, but there is invariably a deep shame connected to it. Perhaps, also, I have met people who are more willing than Alexander and Eugene to talk about their ideas, things that are far more intimate than money and connections, because from what I've noticed, the people I've known in Eugene and Nicole's world are loath to make themselves vulnerable enough to discuss the reality, the content of their art, especially after they suffer some kind of artistic failure. Alexander had talked freely about his first novel with me and with most anyone at the loft on the Bowery, elaborating on its literary interventions, its stylistic experiments, but after this *book project* was rejected by every major publisher, he rarely spoke again about what he was writing about, or even what he was thinking about, even after his next novel was widely celebrated as the new great thing, even as he was poised to become the new Norman Mailer—an apt description, I thought, because his writing was just as solipsistic, self-congratulatory, and mediocre as Mailer's, although it was sexier, perhaps because Alexander had the experience of having once been a very good-looking man and Mailer had not. But even as Alexander's debut novel, which was in fact his second though we weren't allowed to mention that, was widely celebrated, he refused to discuss literature, or even ideas, beyond the fact that he had *met Andrew Wylie for coffee* or that he had *sat next to Sarah Jessica Parker at the Booker Prize ceremony* or that he had *gone with Ben Lerner to pick out a new armchair and wound up with this hideous brown chenille wing chair*, he had said once when I went over to his apartment, *if it weren't for Ben Lerner I would have never bought this hideous wing chair.* Eugene now announced that dinner would be delayed yet further for the actress, and I felt that I should have stayed home and read my Bernhard, that I should have stayed home and read something like *Woodcutters.* I was a fool to have come here when I could have had a better dinner at home, even a dinner of soft-boiled eggs and some inoffensive ambient music from the internet radio station and the Bernhard. I would have eaten better at home than here at the Bowery anticipating whatever avant-gruel I was waiting to be served in the company of the worst vultures in the world.

Nicole and Eugene were, as ever, trapping us all here to distract themselves from the boring monotony of their lives. That was the central tenet of their *hospitality style*. When I lived with Eugene and Nicole, I sometimes felt sorry for them for having everything that they could possibly want without trying. I don't suffer from the Protestant work ethic, but I do think that there is something satisfying about working, about completion. Eugene made art because he wanted the cultural prestige that came with it, obviously, but I think he also made work to keep himself busy. For him, life was a race against the clock to outperform his father (impossible) or at least become something besides his father's son. He was always in his studio working feverishly on his next exhibition, or on a photo spread for one of those six-inch-thick fashion magazines that I'm convinced are money-laundering schemes for Russian oligarchs or fashion brands who made a little too much money in the Gulf or something because I've never heard of anyone *subscribing* to them and yet there they are, replenished biannually at that one magazine store on Eighth Avenue, one of maybe ten places on earth that stocks them, each time full of high production value photo spreads. In any case, Eugene's sense of futility was buried deep beneath a frenzy of activity. It was Nicole I felt sorry for, Nicole, who made nothing, who did nothing. She *curated* but she *did* nothing, nothing but walk from studio visit to studio visit buying artists lunch and buying artists' work and trying to buy herself the feeling of satisfaction that comes from actually doing something. Though I have nothing against inactivity, after a while doing nothing feels almost draining and pathetic. Miraculously I pitied her. Deeply pitied her. She would spend her days basically killing time until the day was over. Her days were for nothing. Her days were for walking around, for lunchtime, for pulling people who were doing something out of their work and into her world of inactivity, into her life of constant distraction. She would run out the clock until it was time to go to bed, hoping that a bright fresh morning would bring meaning to her life, hoping that she would get a good night's sleep so that the next morning she would be ready to get up and do something, that tomorrow's vast expanse of hours would feel like a gift, would blow swiftly by as she was swept up into thinking, into reading, maybe, if she was lucky, into work. I remember the times when I would visit the house in Rhinebeck, when I was ensorcelled by the luxury of that house, the softness of its linens, the limitless tasty and innovative beverages, the uninterrupted green of the view. The nicest place in the house was an office with floor-to-ceiling windows and a low mahogany desk surrounded by pink and orange Mashru silk floor pillows from India. It wasn't Eugene's or Nicole's office, they each had their own. It was just an office. The problem with the office was that it had no door to cordon it off from the rest of the house. It had a long glass wall that blocked out noise but allowed for anyone to see what you were doing from the hallway. Whenever I was at Eugene and Nicole's, I would bring my writing materials— my computer, my notebooks, whatever I was reading—and I would be encouraged to set these things up in the beautiful office. But when I would sit down to write, invariably, Nicole would come and stand by the glass wall and watch me, remark on how cute it was that I was working, on how she didn't want to disturb me, on how she loved to know that I was using her house to fulfill my creative goals. She would say these things and then she would linger there, watching me as I tried to work, occasionally asking if I needed anything to drink or letting me know she planned on lighting the sauna soon or that she was going for a walk and *did I want to join* her. She was doing everything she could to distract me from my work and keep me with her in the world of killing time. It seriously pained me, because when I would wake up at five a.m., before anyone in the house, I would luxuriate in that office, cross-legged on the Mashru pillows, watching the sun come up as I wrote longhand on a legal pad, and then Nicole would come down and realize I'd woken up before her and then feel guilty to have exhibited *some kind of sloth*. Then, for the rest of my stay she would set her alarm so that by the time I got to the office she'd already be in the kitchen with a fresh pot of coffee, reading the newspaper on an iPad, looking for some conversation. It was like I was a zoo animal given its perfect habitat but electrocuted every time I got too comfortable as a reminder to perform for the crowd. I never really got any significant work done up in Rhinebeck, where the conditions were perfect, and so I understood how Nicole felt, given that she too had set her world up perfectly, a grand New York loft, a house in Rhinebeck, property in Europe, but didn't know how to live in it. Of course, I felt lucky to be welcome at the house in Rhinebeck. Even when I moved out of Eugene and Nicole's house and into my own apartment, the summer months in the city were unlivable. I have an incredibly sensitive sense of smell, which is basically a curse if you are interested in living in a city, especially a city like New York that is prone to malodor even without the piles of garbage that line the sidewalks the way I imagine rows of hydrangeas can be found along the streets in standard middle-class suburban areas. In the summer months the city became completely intolerable for me, and so I was grateful to Eugene and Nicole for inviting me to Rhinebeck, where I was reminded of how much more delicious air is that has been filtered through oak trees rather than the eternal blunt wrap of the city. I knew that my friends who were my contemporaries, who didn't have *benefactors* the way I had Eugene and Nicole, were, though they would never admit it, incredibly jealous of my ability to escape the city when it got too sickening. People would pretend that the month of August in the city was the best month because it was *gritty* and *real* and only the *true New Yorkers* were left there, but most of the people saying that had moved to the city from the Midwest or the New Jersey suburbs, and clung tightly to the idea of being *authentic New Yorkers* only because they felt they had to or else they were living a lie. *Real New Yorkers* have been leaving Manhattan every summer since the Dutch or whoever it was landed on the island and started ruining everything. The desire for authentic *New Yorkerhood* drives me crazy because there is no such thing as a *New Yorker*, though there are some people like me who grew up here and because of it thought a *strip mall* was a place for *exotic dancers*, people like me who never learned to drive and are hopeless whenever they're more than five minutes away from a twenty-four-hour pharmacy. But it is not as though being from New York makes them special. It's actually a mental illness to be from New York. It has rendered me completely moronic when it comes to the *great outdoors*, where I routinely do things like lie down in what I think is an idyll but is really a bed of poison ivy concealing a nest of fire ants. As a kid, I seriously thought that the whole earth by default was paved with cement, and *on top of the cement* people had planted grass to make Central Park. When I said this to my mother, I was sent away to an outdoors-based summer camp without electricity where we were made to bathe in a lake. Anyway, the whole population of the city is divided in the summer months into those who have access to somewhere better to go and those who have to pretend that suntanning on a fire escape is glamorous. The *transplants* showed their *transplantiness* most when they didn't know that most people who had lived in the city for generations were desperate to leave during the summer. They usually had at least one summer place they could worm their way into, even if it was totally crap, and if they didn't they were searching for one at all times. But the young people I knew tried to make *summer in the city* seem like the most intoxicating hedonistic fun that could possibly be had, like it was an *unmissable thrill*, and the more they tried to convince me of this, just the way that when a friend messages you many times throughout the night to come to a party because it is *really fun* you know it's a disaster, the more I knew how lucky I was to be transported to

Rhinebeck. Though then you had to take into account the particular hell of that house, which was that when you were alone, you were in paradise, because it was so wonderfully air-conditioned and conducive to comfort and serenity, but when you were with Nicole, you were expected to completely subordinate your own desires to hers. You had to eat when she wanted to, make excursions to lakes and antique shops and farm stands when she wanted to, you had to play a game or watch a film or worse yet have a conversation whenever it convenienced her, and all at the same time you had to indulge her lightly in that conversation, you had to encourage her for her quick wit, concede to her point of view in debate, praise her for her taste and her cooking all without seeming too simpering, of course, because if she was made to feel like she was being pandered to Nicole would cut you out completely. She was your *benefactress* but she was also your friend. Nicole had serious paranoia because though she always felt supported and loved by those around her, she couldn't trust that love and support if her suspicion that she was being played for her money was correct, and she knew that it was, which led her to snap and snarl and yell at her houseguests. I knew one man who was never invited back to Rhinebeck after he went on a nature walk with Nicole and an artist called Clara Carson and me, maybe Rebecca was there too, and he praised Nicole too much for her knowledge of plant and tree species on the walk and when we got back to the house she told us all he was a *pathetic little flatterer*, and we all agreed that he was *pathetic*, but what Nicole clearly hadn't realized was that she had created an entire social world around her that was ruled by flattering her *just enough* so that she didn't notice, and that Rebecca and Clara and I were actually working *much harder* to flatter Nicole without her knowing. But really the worst part about being in the house at Rhinebeck was the feeling that you were unable to go home because you relied on them for transportation, because they so kindly drove you up there from the city, so there was a sense of being a captive with no control over your body, and yet your body was in supreme comfort. Of course, the reality of Nicole's gilded birdcage was that, even more than trapping us, it made *her* detest us all. It complicated her friendships with everyone, because she felt, in the back of her mind, like we were only ever taking from her, like all we did was take from her—like we were there not because we loved her or even liked her but because she had things that we wanted. And to a certain degree that was true, but it was something that only *became* true because she had pushed us away and all that was left to demonstrate closeness were the things. At one point, I recalled as I sat watching her sitting at the head of the table, gesticulating wildly in a way that was a dead giveaway she was *being political*, at one point I had thought Nicole was the most fantastic person on earth, and that her generosity was just part of her overall benevolence. But then suddenly the generosity always came with a wink, and then a scowl. If you declined the things she pushed on you, you were ungrateful, but if you took them you loved her for her things alone, even if you really did love her because she was actually quite hilarious, uninhibited, and kind. There was no one who suffered from this dynamic more than Eugene, who she had trapped most thoroughly with her money and her comfort. There was no one she had given more gifts to; she gave the gift of an entire lifestyle to Eugene. So because of this there was no one she detested more than her partner, Eugene, who of course at one point had loved Nicole so much that he gave up his life of bachelor freedom to cohabitate with her, but she could never trust that his love was sincerely about *her* exactly because she came with a lot of other things that were very appealing. Was it her fault that she wanted to and *could* give Eugene everything he had ever wanted? She gave him the house, which was ruined somehow because it was mostly hers, she gave him the vacations, which were ruined because they were *her* vacations—*she* picked the places and even when she didn't, *she* picked the hotels, *she* picked the restaurants. Even his art practice wasn't left untouched by Nicole's money because she provided all the money for their lives, and so he was able to pay for more studio assistants to make his work, and even though he paid their salaries, he knew it was only possible through *not* having to pay for other things. So eventually he began to resent Nicole, he began to hate that people thought of him as a *kept man* when his father had been *self-made*. He began to hate that though he was *successful* everyone knew where the *real money* came from. And in turn, Nicole hated Eugene because she could never be sure if he loved her or her money. She was often jealous of the young *pieces of ass* that Eugene brought into their lives, not because she was possessive or because she thought that Eugene loved these women more than her, but because she wished that for once she could know that the only reason someone wanted to fuck her was because she was a hot piece of ass. I allowed myself to glance across the room at Alexander, who I had been trying my hardest not to look at for the duration of the evening. His face, which had always been gaunt and topographical, had flattened. His once long, thin nose seemed to have spread out wider across his face, and the hollows under his cheekbones were filled in with flesh and bloat. Not only had Alexander disfigured his already ghoulish appearance— Rebecca always said that alcohol-drinking was the number one cause of ugliness and disfiguration, followed by cocaine-taking, which was why she stuck to the benzodiazepines and opioids, which had the added benefit of helping her remain trim—but Alexander's outfits clearly had become more elaborately shabby. This wasn't because Alexander wasn't successful. He had written a novel that was well reviewed in the *Times* and was being made into a film by one of New York's most prominent producers. I could be sure he was eager to discuss this with the film producer who was sitting on an Italian modernist pony-hair chair, looking down at his phone between his legs, which were spread out as if he was taking up two seats on the subway. Though Alexander would of course need the producer to recognize *him* and bring up the film deal, which was unlikely to occur. No, Alexander's clothes had remained shabby in keeping with his idea of himself as a *serious person*. I knew, however, that he obsessed over what other people wore. I remember maybe seven years ago we were at a party, Alexander and I, and he saw a woman he was interested in talking to some guy across the room and he said, *that loser in Acne jeans*, he really said, *she's talking to that loser in Acne jeans*. He could recognize the designer of a pair of jeans from across a room *and* form some negative opinion of the wearer based on the brand name alone, and yet he still maintained that he was *agnostic about fashion*, that he *didn't notice clothing*. Or actually I now remember he had said to me once *I don't see jewelry when people wear it*, when I asked him if he thought I should buy a silver necklace I saw in a window we walked past he said, *I don't see jewelry when people wear it*, as if he was such an intellectually and spiritually pure person that he couldn't even perceive material things, and yet he could recognize the make of a pair of jeans from across a room *and* pass some judgment on a sexual rival from it. This was the man who found it appalling the way *serious people* spent so much of their *mental energy* on fashion. The same Alexander who, in the four-hour interval between Rebecca's beachside funeral and the dinner had changed out of his black suit and into the uniform I recognized him in: a brown and gray tweed suit that I suspected was the one he had bought from the well-stocked thrift store near Nicole's beach house in Montauk. It had never occurred to me until now, as I sat on the sofa after Rebecca's funeral, that Alexander had spent so much of his life wearing a dead man's Brooks Brothers suit. I hadn't had time to go back home and change out of what I had worn to the funeral, and now I felt somewhat ridiculous, sitting in my black silk skirt and black cotton blouse under a black wool sweater that I dared not remove, though I was getting hot as I sat on the corner seat of the sofa, realizing I had finished at least three glasses of the orange wine, my glass having never gone empty because Alexander, with his middle-class manners, always made a big show of refilling glasses for the women, especially when someone else had paid for the wine. I was hot but I dared not take off my black sweater even though I began to feel a redness effervesce up from my trunk onto my cheeks, because I knew I had sweat-stained armpits because I was the only one who had not changed out of my funeral clothes and into something different for the dinner. I was the only one that dared to wear black to a dinner that may as well have been Rebecca's wake, or her shiva or whatever Rebecca's Italian-American ancestors call it when your closest friends get together to pretend you never even existed and talk about their movie projects and solo shows as they hang about and devise schemes for mid-level social climbing as if you had not just died. I was the only one who had bothered to continue wearing my black clothes, though I had to admit it was in part because I hadn't felt like taking the subway all the way back uptown to my grandmother's apartment to change into something else. Though, had I known the actress still wouldn't have arrived by half past ten, and that the actual eating of dinner would be this late, I might have gone up and changed, but I'm convinced that unlike Alexander I wouldn't have put on my New York School shabby-prep cosplay uniform of a dead man's brown tweed threadbare suit. And unlike Nicole I wouldn't have squeezed myself into that tight purple skirt that showed off her legs, the stumpiness of which had only increased since the last time I'd seen her. Her calves had swollen and her once shapely figure had, over these past five years, lost its elegant serpentine shape, her body's contours averaged, flattened, into a brick. Eugene, of course, had worn his bright blue beret and orange puffer jacket to the funeral, and I admired him for not even attempting to conceal who he really was, to pretend that he was not a self-involved predacious remora, a suckling ravening piranha, he really did look like a fish sometimes, yes, I admired him for being honest that for even one afternoon it was impossible for him to not *dress*. I had even overheard Eugene at the funeral saying to one of the young people they had brought along that *Rebecca would have wanted us all in our brights*. I had never seen Rebecca wear a bright color in her life. She was always in black and white, in antique white petticoats and chemises, or threadbare white Edwardian corset covers with black ballet tights as pants, like Edie Sedgwick. But in a sense, I appreciated Eugene's self-knowledge, his unwillingness to deceive people into thinking that he cared enough to wear black to the funeral, unlike his partner, who had worn her ridiculous black Margiela mourning costume. Eugene was admittedly a genius for a certain kind of self-presentation. One of the things I learned from him was to pretend to not be as calculating as I really was, as eager as I really was, because seeming like you actually want things you don't have is the surest way to be denied them. Eugene understood that if you turned things that you desperately wanted into horrible obligations, people would be more likely to give them to you. Whenever Eugene wanted to work with a new gallery, for instance, his first move was always to stealthily manage to run into its director in a way that seemed purely coincidental, and then complain about invented collectors who had pre-bought his works for his next show before the date was even set. He would complain and say that he didn't even really feel like having a show, that he was so over going to openings and speaking to people and feeling like a used car salesman when all he really was interested in was holing up in his studio and working, but that it was so hard to turn down his *devoted collectors* who had supported him throughout his career, and to *leave them hanging* now would be just as bad as *leaving his gallery* who had guided him through the bloodsucking art world for so long, and he would never dream of doing that, he would never dream of deserting his gallery that had nurtured his artistic talent from its most pathetic attempts at image-making to his current fully realized intellectual works. How could he leave a gallery that had helped him maintain such a successful sales record, a record that included institutions and collectors in equal measure? It would be difficult to leave a gallery like that, Eugene would say, so he just had to slog through making these last works, which of course was a delight but was somehow cheapened by knowing that collectors had pre-bought them. It felt as if he were a short-order cook flipping burgers and whisking omelets for people who had already ordered them, because he knew what each collector would want so clearly, that instead of working as a chef, dictating what would be on the menu for his gallery show, he was working to make his collectors happy since there was no point in doing anything but *satiate their appetites.* The gallerist, of course, would hear this brazen self-promotional rant disguised as a complaint and offer him a show at their gallery, because it's never a bad thing to have an artist with so many devoted collectors, and Eugene's work was just bland enough to fit in with most programs. He did this twice, to my knowledge. The first time to secure representation with a very nice, if a bit boring, gallery in Brussels, and again to level up from his small-but-respectable New York digs to one of the Chelsea behemoths. Of course, he could have done it a few more times in my absence, but I haven't made it a point to *follow his career closely.* But Eugene taught me to avoid stating my ambitions clearly, in fact I learned from him to say the opposite of what I thought: to talk down about any magazine that I desperately wanted to publish in, to ridicule anyone who was successful in exactly the way I wanted to be for their *brazen careerism.* It was a brilliant form of misdirection, but all it amounted to for me was the feeling that I should be jealous of people I didn't even care that much about. I blamed this attitude I'd imbibed from Eugene—that of wanting things that people I didn't respect had for the sole reason that I imagined myself to be better than them—for kickstarting my short-lived *career* in fashion magazines. The first job I'd gotten writing for these magazines was from a middle-aged woman with a child's name. I had met her at a dinner at the Bowery shortly after the premiere of the film I wrote with Rebecca, and she had seen the film *at a screening,* she told me, *not on the computer,* she told me, she *didn't believe in streaming things,* she told me, she *still believed in seeing things in theater*, she told me, she *had never owned a television*, she told me, she *still believed in seeing things in theater*, she had said. She worked at a major fashion publication, a magazine that *set the fashion conversation*, she had said, rolling her eyes, I remembered, as I sat on the corner seat of the sofa. She had rolled her eyes when she told me the title of the famous magazine where she was a high-ranking editor, as if to say, though I am responsible for the content, tone, and voice of this magazine I have *nothing to do with it*. I remembered too that she wore no makeup in a way that was *different* from the way that other women in the artistic world wore no makeup. I had noticed that other women in the artistic world—like Nicole, who was her *dear friend*—wore a small amount of makeup that highlighted their natural beauty, concealing any imperfections. They maintained a stringent dermatological regimen that allowed them to wear no makeup and look, as the phrase from advertisements that made my head want to explode would have it, *lit from within*. But I remembered that the magazine editor with the child's name wore *not a shred* of makeup. She was, of course, strikingly beautiful and yet she allowed her face to be *sallow*, *wrinkled*, and *drawn* like a normal human face. She *wore no makeup* and she *had no television*, and yet she actually managed both of these things in a way that I found to be unaffected; I too did not own a television, nor did I wear makeup, but of course I was in my early twenties and did not have many possessions, or even an apartment, nor was I a high-ranking editor at one of the most important fashion magazines in the country. I think I may have noticed the absence of makeup, however, because her face actually looked a lot like mine, the magazine editor with the child's name, and I wonder if it was because she noticed this resemblance herself that she took an immediate interest in me, inviting me to the offices of the fashion magazine, which really were as sleek as they'd been portrayed in the novels and films set there. A tall, thin woman who *really was wearing stiletto heels to work* shuttled me through an antiseptic white hallway full of other stiletto heel wearers into the magazine editor's office and then we were alone together sequestered within her glass-walled office, about the size of a handicap-accessible bathroom at a Starbucks, stuffed with high-fashion ephemera—runway sketches with inscriptions made out to her by famous dead designers, gift bags from fashion houses, framed photos of her posed with supermodels, the day's mail, boxes from beauty brands, boxed sneakers, boxed lingerie, a box of new protein bars manufactured by a video-blogger-slash-boxer, a gold vase with an arrangement of peonies and anthuriums with a large card affixed to the front inviting the editor to a runway show, and a mason jar full of what appeared to be a green milkshake but on further inspection was a green curry sent as promotional material for a Thai shoe designer's new cookbook. As I waited for the editor to finish a phone call, I noticed also that on the wall, next to a cardboard cutout of Karl Lagerfeld wearing a birthday hat, was a bookshelf full of books from a major left-wing publishing house, and I wondered what those were doing there, and she saw me looking at them and immediately told me they were from a *previous life* when she worked in left-wing political organizing, from a *previous life*, she said, *before I traded in dialectical materialism for straight materialism*, she had said to me in the office, and she gestured out at the rows of young women sitting at their cubicles clacking out articles about *reissues of old Chanel purses*, articles about what *celebrities wore to the gym*. But even though she *felt far more comfortable in the art world*, she said, *and even more comfortable around academics*, she said, she did *this*—and here she waved her hand around her office—because she *truly loved fashion*. It was *embedded somewhere inside* of her to *really love the clothes*, and so she suffered little knowing that she supervised one woman whose job consisted of writing four-hundred-word articles about every single outfit Kim Kardashian wore, which would *never have happened before the rise of digital*, she said, *never before the rise of digital*, she repeated to me as we sat in her office, but *digital was a gift*, she said, for someone *deeply interested in studying the semiotics of fashion, and wasn't Instagram, wasn't Kim Kardashian a gift, an unusual opportunity to see what captivates the minds of most people?* But none of that was what had interested her in fashion, really. She ended up here because of her *love of beautiful things*, which she conceded would be, to most people, *surprising, given the background in Marxist thought*, she said, narrowing her eyes at me as if to emphasize the crow's-feet that she had accumulated from a life lived virtuously, free of fillers and expensive eye cream. But her *background in Marxist thought* should not preclude her from *a life devoted to beauty*, she said, defensively, although I had not spoken for fifteen minutes. She leaned back in her Aeron chair and said, *I believe that everyone should have access to beautiful things*, she said, *that is why I am so devoted to magazines, so that for the cover price, everyone can have access to beautiful things.* I had assumed that she had summoned me there to offer me a writing assignment or a job or something, but instead I was probed for about thirty minutes about my relationship to Eugene and how I'd gotten to know Alexander, and then she asked me about what books I was reading, what films I had seen recently. She asked me if I had been to the theater at all lately, and she tried to find out things about my education—if I had been privately educated, if my college had been prestigious *and* culturally relevant, or just prestigious, if I had grown up with *intellectuals*, or if my parents had lots of money, or if they were the kinds of intellectuals who were able to be intellectuals because they had lots of money. I felt no shame in answering any of these questions about myself, though I bent the truth slightly toward what I thought she wanted to hear. I did however feel an odd friction between us. I felt, in fact, an incredible sense of unease while speaking to her. She was quiet when someone else would have replied, which led me to speak ineloquently and continue beyond the point when I should have stopped speaking, and then she interrupted when someone else would have been quiet, which made me feel as if I had begun to ramble. She spoke with a censorious quality that disarmed me, that made me feel as if I had done something wrong by sitting in her office, as if I had forced my way in and interrupted her work—and then I remembered that she had invited me there, and I then remembered to ask her why it was she had brought me here, and eventually she said that she wanted me to write a few articles about fashion in an interesting way for her, that she had seen the film I made with Rebecca and thought *that is somebody I'd like to have in the magazine*. And so she offered me a contract writing articles for the magazine and I accepted and was then brought into another office, where the head of operations explained what I would be paid per article, and I accepted even though I knew that if I calculated the hourly wage I would earn from writing for one of the biggest fashion magazines in the world it would be something comparable to what I could expect to make as a laborer in a diamond mine or in a country where they send the Super Bowl T-shirts they printed for the losing team, and I mean that literally, I would be paid in pennies per hour for my writing, and of course there would be no health insurance benefits, though I would be contracted to write a set number of pieces per day, which meant that I couldn't really expect to be able to devote any time to working elsewhere, and now I understood why all the women who worked in the cubicles had perfect hair and skin and wore stiletto shoes because they could *afford to take cabs to the office*, because the *office* was more like a *day care* for them to while away the hours, and I accepted the rate because I could continue living at Nicole and Eugene's and because I too had nothing better to do, I mean, I wasn't all that different from the girls in the stilettos, when I really thought about it, just I'd had to debase myself repeatedly and in sickening ways for my lifestyle of ease. I wondered if any of them had to do the same. I was then returned to the editor's office, where I asked if she could do anything about the pathetic rate that I was offered, and I now recalled she had said, when I told her they had offered me a rate of one-quarter what an online art magazine had paid me for a review I had written, *that any article she published would be read by one hundred times the number of people as that article*. It was clear that she had intended this to be a consolation for the pittance that they would pay for a thousand-word article rather than an underscoring of the patently exploitative structure of the magazine that she worked for, where editors had gifts from designers—thousand-dollar handbags, luxury lingerie— piled up like garbage in their offices, though hers were next to *books*, like an advance copy of a new edition of *The Prison Notebooks* coming out in a few months with an introduction by a sort-of-annoying soft-left intellectual I was eager to read and make fun of with Alexander. I wrote five articles for the magazine at that rate before I got sick of being edited by the junior editor who revised my sentences *into* the passive voice, who excised any cultural references more complicated than *it's like Disney*, and who sent me into a minor cardiac episode when I flipped to see an article I had written *revised* to include multiple uses of the phrase *flirty frocks*. During this period, the middle-aged fashion editor with the child's name had disappeared from the office along with the more elegant editrixes, for *fashion month*, and from Paris and London and Milan she responded to zero of my messages, which asked if she had *time to speak*, because I was too afraid to write in an email that she needed to get the junior editor to stop messing with my articles. That if they insisted on paying me practically nothing, they should at the very least give me control over the words that were attached to my name, phrases like *statement bauble* that I would not like to have an *indelible record* of having written, especially when I had not. I really was going to lose my mind with that. Statement bauble. And so I stopped responding to the emails I got from the magazine in the middle of my sixth round of edits with the overbearing and stupid subeditor on a piece about a jeweler who, according to this editor, made *contemporary heirlooms*, which made no sense to me because the very point of an heirloom is that it is passed down from generation to generation, so what was the point of writing that they were *contemporary heirlooms*, did that not just mean recently purchased expensive things to eventually be left to a daughter? No one is expected to *throw their jewelry in the garbage* because it was made in this century. Instead I wanted to write about the fact that the jewelry designer had grown up on a sailing ship in the middle of the Atlantic Ocean, which she had mentioned to me casually during the phone interview, an interview she spent mostly maligning other jewelry designers she knew personally, whose successes apparently accounted for her lack of sales and poor media coverage, although I was literally interviewing her at that moment, but the subeditor didn't like my sailing angle, she was focused on the idea that the jewelry designer's pieces were *contemporary heirlooms*, and as I began writing the piece that I was assigned, writing sentence after sentence without referent, spinning words into nothing until I reached the bottom of the page, somehow having gotten to the point where I had of my own free will written the phrase *the jewelry yearns to be cherished*, I wrote in to the subeditor that I would no longer be coming into the office. I wrote nothing to the editor with the child's name, because I had figured that she wouldn't reply, as she hadn't to the other emails that I had sent her attempting to finagle a living wage from the magazine while she was in Paris and London and Milan viewing the fashion shows. I didn't see her until years later, just before I left the city, at a political rally for the left-wing candidate for president that I attended with some friends who hosted a podcast about politics and online culture that I had never listened to, but was clearly very popular because we were given excellent seats in the press section and I had to take many photos of the presidential candidate's staffers with the podcasters, which made me feel curious about the podcast but not curious enough to debase myself by listening to it. Midway through the rally, I saw the magazine editor, during the speech of a young politician stumping for the presidential candidate, a young politician who had repositioned himself as a queer Democratic Socialist after demonstrating against abortion at his Ivy League university, something I had to remind myself was completely acceptable, that not everyone had grown up with parents who forced three-part Trotsky biographies on friends you brought home from school, and that even I had imbibed some of my father's vague and hypocritical pro-war hawkish sentiments when I was younger. Though when it came to the politician things were far more severe; I was told by a friend who had gone to college with him that the politician had lied to his boyfriend and many of his friends at school about having a rare form of cancer, which began when the boyfriend had tried to break up with him, and after he'd staved off the breakup with the cancer it must have seemed like such an appealing and useful lie that his *cancer* had progressed to a stage in which he would use it as an excuse to get out of exams and cleaning and social obligations, and even, and this was a rumor but it was so specific that I had no choice but to believe it, began asking people to drive him to chemotherapy sessions so that they would drop him off in places that were convenient when he needed a ride somewhere, a practice that was only uncovered when someone who had just dropped the politician off at what they believed was Sloan Kettering discovered him getting a pedicure. Everyone, however, does unsavory things in their youth. I had decided to believe the cancer myth was a rumor spread by a jealous spurned lover, especially as the politician had since dropped his fervent pro-life conservative routine and devoted himself to prison reform and winning universal health care and a whole score of other noble and unglamorous causes I didn't even know about. So I had decided that I liked him because it was braver to try to enter spaces that may reject you for your past misdeeds and become a better person than it was to sink further into perdition, to be embraced with open arms by the right wing, by those who applaud dishonesty and actively try to make the world a less habitable place. While I was listening to the politician speak I heard a familiar voice in the background, and I turned around, and speaking to a famous boomer known for her left-wing organizing and fantastic breasts was the magazine editor with the child's name, who made eye contact with me in a way that unnerved me in the same way that conversations with her always had because I wasn't sure what her tone was, if she was trying to be complimentary or cutting, just as now I was unsure if she wanted to convey that she liked me and was glad to see me or hoped that by looking at me I would melt away or die. All I knew was that her eyes were sort of squinty. But her eyes always seemed a bit squinty, or maybe they were just small eyes. While the politician talked, however, I felt protected from whatever authority the magazine editor had. I was flanked by left-wing micro-celebrities, in the center of a crowd in which their cachet trumped hers. In fact her mainstream corporate media credentials probably made her feel like an outsider at the political event even though she wanted to reminisce about her *left-wing publishing* bona fides; her past political experience probably just made her more aware of the futility and wastefulness of her consumerist profession in the eyes of the attendees and so I decided that I would approach her. Perhaps because I wanted to use the moment in which I believed that I had the upper hand to reverse the circumstances of our previous meeting at the fashion magazine, in which I had felt so powerless and used by her all while being completely overlooked, or perhaps for some other purpose that is obscure to me now, but probably involved what Eugene would call *networking*. And so when I approached her she said *oh, of course you're here*, but not in a sarcastic tone, I could tell that she meant *you and I are the same, and wherever I am, wherever I am that I feel most myself, that's where*

*I would expect you to be*, because I'm sure that when she was at fashion shows and at galas and at charity functions filled with fashion people she would look around and think *I am different from these people. I am not really here, I am here as an emissary from the world of intellectuals and I write about and make sense of your world in a way that you do not understand*, but here at the left-wing presidential candidate's campaign rally she thought *this is who I really am, and none of the people I see at the galas and the fashion shows and the charity functions are here, but I am here, surrounded by the people who are like me*, and so when she said *of course you're here*, I could tell she meant this as something like a compliment and I felt humiliated by my pride at being in the press-slash-VIP section of the left-wing presidential candidate's campaign rally and my pride that she should notice that I was with a certain kind of *left-wing podcasting micro-celebrity* instead of in the cramped and sweaty general area with the *regular campaign supporters* when the entire reason that I admired the presidential candidate was his pledge to take on corporations and billionaires who believed that because of their ability to wield influence and power they were better than other people, and *who did I really think I was*. The magazine editor with the child's name asked me if I was *still writing*, which alluded to our business dealings in a way that was just oblique enough to not invite a conversation about it but just *rude* enough, I mean the implication that I would *quit writing* because I hadn't found it fulfilling to write for her fashion magazine, and I felt like an idiot for answering simply *sure*. We didn't talk about Eugene and Nicole, I hadn't seen them for over a year, and I hadn't seen her at one of their *evenings* for longer than that. I'd only heard her name mentioned when, a few years before I stopped talking to Eugene, he had tried and succeeded in lobbying the editor for an invitation to one of the magazine's celebrity-packed parties, an elegant dinner aboard the Circle Line, where guests dripped candles made from butter on radish rosettes and ate smoked trout on knäckebröd under the Statue of Liberty and Eugene, between bottles of salty Catalan sparkling water, sold two sculptures to a B-list actress and had spent months extolling the actress's *great taste* and *subtle beauty* until Nicole said in a soft, deep, quite unnerving voice that she knew he had slept with the actress and she didn't need to be reminded of it, and Eugene had denied it in a way that made it clear he wanted her to know he had, which made me believe that it was a total fabrication, that Nicole had concocted this so-called affair with an actress in order to prolong the lie she had long been telling herself about Eugene's desirability, and Eugene, of course, had adamantly denied the affair in order to make it seem all the more true. I thought about bringing all of this up to the magazine editor to see if she had any insight into the situation but I didn't want my idle curiosity to give her any fuel for the furnace of her own self-satisfaction, even if it was only at the expense of Eugene and Nicole. The politician had stopped speaking and now the presidential candidate's campaign manager took the stage wearing a bright red brocade blazer and the magazine editor with the child's name told me that she was considering assigning a piece on the campaign manager, who was just *fabulous*, and I agreed with her, she was *fabulous*, and we agreed that we really did like her red brocade blazer, and I felt better about the magazine editor, because in the midst of writing for her about *fabulous flirty frocks* I had lost sight of the fact that perhaps she really was using her job at one of the nation's biggest fashion magazines to bring mainstream awareness to left-wing political concerns—perhaps *The Prison Notebooks* had been on her desk not as a vestige of her old life but as a conscious reminder that she could do something about *hegemony* using the fashion media, that she could change people's politics using *cultural production*. I smiled to myself, satisfied that perhaps my time at the magazine had not been wasted, and then I wondered if I could get myself assigned to that story about the campaign manager, but I thought better of it, and then she complimented me on my outfit and I took that as a cue to leave and I didn't see her again until Rebecca's memorial service. She had met Rebecca a handful of times at parties at Nicole and Eugene's house and when I saw her there, at the memorial, she told me she had *greatly admired Rebecca*, she had *greatly admired the small works of hers that she had seen*, the things that she had been *lucky enough to be able to witness*. I found that a bit rich, given that she'd met Rebecca maybe four times, but then everyone loves to exaggerate their closeness to dead people, they love to imagine how close they *would have been* with the dead person if only they'd managed to live a bit longer so their schedules could sync up better. In just a few years they might have had a standing weekly lunch. Lots of people at the funeral barely knew Rebecca, because she was the sort of extremely minor downtown celebrity who it is much chicer to know and thereby to grieve for than an actual public figure in the mainstream. The magazine editor had turned up at the memorial with a large bouquet of waxy black lilies that she carried around the beach aimlessly, and from the troubled look on her face it seemed that she had no idea what to do with. There was no coffin or grave to lay the flowers on, and everyone was organized in a sort of rhizomatic blob structure without even any *front* where she could lay the flowers so that people could see her paying her respects vis-à-vis the flowers, and so I watched as she carried the large arrangement of black cascading lilies around the beach as Emily circulated the baggie of Rebecca's ashes. I watched as the magazine editor clutched the flowers to her chest with one arm as she accepted a handful of the ashes in a sort of awkward, distant motion, and when the instructions came to scatter the ashes she was careful to keep the debris away from her person, she tossed them sort of behind her head so that the wind wouldn't carry them back into her face, so that Rebecca wouldn't slap her in the face, and all the while she was clutching the flowers into her chest, protecting the flowers from the ashes. She had, early in the memorial, between the ash scattering and Alexander's long speech, approached me in her usual way, in a way that made me feel as though *I* had come over to her and inconvenienced her. She'd squinted at me as if she didn't recognize me while *she* approached *me*, she made her awkward quizzical face for long enough that she forced me to speak first and say her name as if I had approached her to say hello to her, and she said *yes, hello, of course you're here*, she said to me at Rebecca's memorial, *of course you're here*, she repeated. *Are you still writing?* I nodded at her and didn't say anything because I felt the way she was behaving was humiliating, that she had greeted me the same way she did at the political rally—that she was turning Rebecca's memorial, someone who *wasn't famous* but *all the right people knew*, a person she barely knew, into the same kind of event, one at which it was important to register your attendance, that your attendance showed the other attendees that you were the *right kind of person*. So I nodded at her but didn't even smile because I felt she was using the small things she had over me to lay a trap for me to debase myself. There's a certain kind of person who is expert in dangling their connections, their social clout, in front of you so that you feel both disgusting for associating with them because it would appear that you're attempting to take advantage of them, but also guilty if you snub them, because perhaps they are not just the web of social ties that you've cruelly made them out to be—and this, of course, is why Eugene was once so in with the magazine editor with the child's name, because she commissioned a series of photographs from him for her magazine, and he invited her everywhere in order to secure future highly paid work for the magazine that would also afford him access to models and A-list actresses. But after that one spread she never offered him any photography work again, and this was the genius of the magazine editor, this insured that she would be invited to each and every party that Eugene had, that she would be given access to more of his friends, like me, who she had gotten to write for her, and like Rebecca, whose young model friends she was after. She had, according to Nicole, once enticed Rebecca with the promise of assigning a writer to cover her *little show* but had never followed through with it as Rebecca's show had *closed so soon* that there was *no reason to write about it now* as *no one could even see it*. She really made me sick, the magazine editor with the child's name, the *comrade* who was so happy to be spotted in the *VIP section* of the left-wing rally in Queens. I could see her thinking, *these people are frivolous, they are the frivolous friends of a frivolous person who died because her life had become unbearably frivolous*, whereas in her mind, the magazine editor's mind, her own life could never be truly frivolous because she *knew* that she had *given up dialectical materialism for straight materialism*. She was impenetrable because she believed that she was studying the machinations of capitalism from its very center—however ridiculous she became she was able to tell herself, *what a wonderful service I am doing to the intellectual community*, however low she became, however embroiled in the world of consumerism and cultural decay, she felt like she was a secret agent, an emissary from the *world of ideas* into the depths of the discount underwear bin, and that was why in that moment I realized maybe she bothered me even more than Eugene and Nicole, who had so brazenly used culture to their own ends in order to surround themselves with people they thought were important, to launder their money and their reputations through *the cultural arts*. Eugene and Nicole knew inside that they were frauds, I thought as I sat in the corner seat of the sofa, they knew that they were completely ridiculous people. That they still needed to throw *cultural evenings* was proof that they were so insecure about their place in the *cultural world* that they felt the only way to remain a part of it was to entice people into their home and ply them with luxuries, dangle their immense wealth, their wrought iron floor-to-ceiling window mullions and their *early* Raymond Pettibon and their disgusting, disgusting unbelievably comfortable and tasteful furniture. They needed to soothe themselves at night with thoughts of how so-and-so sculptor had been to dinner just the other night, and they were *really close friends with* whatever theater director was written up in the Sunday Arts section of the *Times* that they read while they soothed their hangovers and listened to the *people* cleaning up the morning after they'd hosted whoever it was in New York that they were afraid would move past them, whoever they were afraid was about to dominate the cultural sphere without knowing who they were, I thought as I sat on the corner seat of the sofa, watching Nicole talk to some young person with a buzzed head. The magazine editor, meanwhile, though she had an enormous and sleek apartment designed by her former partner, an architect who was part of a powerful group of gay women Nicole called *the celesbians*—I'd never been, I only knew about it because the kitchen was featured in one of the small, arty interior design magazines I read at the delicious lunch restaurant whose irresistible green Mexican soup was, in many ways, the only reason I was back on the Bowery—she never had big parties. She had no reason to. She knew she was to be invited everywhere, and though she was

invited she more often than not did not go because she felt so
secure in her position as an arbiter of cultural taste that she believed that wherever she went became more important by the
value of her presence, and while she was at Rebecca's memorial
service, I am sure that she thought Rebecca would have been
proud to know that she had been there, that she would have felt
like she had *arrived* to know that the magazine editor was at her
funeral. So it was incredibly delicious when, after Alexander had
read his speech to the crowd, Eugene began to make his way
over to her, smiling widely at the sight of her—even at this memorial service, I had thought, Eugene still behaved like a
worm—and I was unsure which one of them would disgust me
more, to watch their conspiratorial sadness, and I was watching
as Eugene approached her, and the wind was quite loud but they
were close to me and he said to her in a very loud voice so that
everyone could hear, *is it true*, he shouted as she clutched her
flowers, *is it true that you're working for Palantir?* And I watched
as the magazine editor with the child's name looked at her feet
and mumbled some things that I couldn't hear. I imagined she
was saying *it's incredibly interesting to see a system that shapes so
much of our lives from the inside*, or, *what a wonderful opportunity it
is to get to peer into the lives of most people through their shopping
data, an opportunity art and even fashion never really afford*, or,
some excuse like *my mother's retirement home is expensive*, though
to her credit this was incredibly unlikely because I doubt she
would stoop so low as to use personal excuses for her behavior;
hiding behind an infirm parent, even one I'd just imagined,

would require her to veer away from her *intellectual motivations*. There was a wide, doleful look in her eyes, which were usually so sharp, so tightly pinched, and I felt a bit vindicated to see her almost *afraid of Eugene*, that she was *afraid of Eugene's judgment*, that *Eugene* had *something over her*, that someone as low as *Eugene* could have something over *her*, but then I felt sick, I realized as I sat in the corner seat of the sofa, I felt totally sick, and I couldn't tell why, I felt an unbearable loss of something I hadn't realized I was losing until just now. I hadn't thought about how much I needed the magazine editor with the child's name, not because I needed her professionally but because, without realizing it, I had turned her into a beacon of reason, of good behavior. I hadn't realized how much I had invested in her life that I knew so little about, how much more depth and meaning and virtue and power I had once given her than she really ever had. I had laughed at her contradictions, at her commodity fetishism and her Marxist politics, because *I believed that I could share in her contradictions*— that she was a model that I had aspired to for living in the world. I had invested energy into believing that she was a rare person who could be obsessed with beautiful things but also interested in making the world a less terrible place, that she could actually escape from the solipsism of the world of art and fashion even while her life was *about* coveting beautiful objects, that she, without a television, was a person who took things seriously, and because of this I had been afraid of her—afraid of her judgments about me, about Eugene and Nicole, about Rebecca, afraid of the way she compared herself to me because I *wanted her to be right.* I wanted her to be *different from them* so that *I could be different from them too.* I *wanted her to be incorruptible* even as she was living a completely contradictory life. But, as she'd joked in her office, she really had *abandoned dialectical materialism for straight materialism,* I thought, as I sat on the corner seat of the sofa, and I had felt a sort of regret as I watched her leave the memorial service. I had believed that I would see her here tonight, I thought as I sat in the corner seat of the sofa at Eugene's, and I imagined that I would be able to speak with her, that maybe it had all been a mistake, that she could defend herself to me. That it was just for research and she was planning on writing some kind of tell-all. Or even maybe she could give me a good reason for working at a corporation in bed with the surveillance state that churns through people's data and sells it to enrich other corporations. No, I wanted to defend *myself* to her, I wanted to show her that I was *nothing* like her, that I had left New York not because I could not become like her but because I *would not,* because I *refused to,* I thought, and I pictured her leaving the memorial service, skulking away just after she had allowed herself to be humiliated by Eugene, her tail between her legs just after she had let one of the stupidest people in the world get the best of her. I remembered the way she called the car on her phone and waited for it, the arrogance of her purposefully unbrushed hair at the memorial service, the crisp, pristine, and simple black wool jacket she crunched up as she clutched the big bouquet of black lilies—and I realized now that she was still holding them, when she left the beach and got into a car, she was still holding

the flowers that she had brought for Rebecca but didn't know
where to leave for the maximum praise. She had left the memorial service *with the flowers*. After the ash-throwing performance
everyone else who had attended the funeral had descended on
the diner near the beach, streaming into the 1950s-style chrome-
sided restaurant in their black, wispy, scrappy clothes that were
in fashion, tattered raggedy expensive shrouds, that streamed
behind them in the wind ghoulishly as they invaded the diner
like the insuppressible wave of crows in *The Birds* who settle,
slowly, bird by bird, on the *jungle gym*, building in their numbers
to a *full murder* before they descend as a monolith, clawing at the
schoolchildren's faces. I walked behind the crowd, staring at the
rocks beside the ocean bathed in that midwinter slanty orange
light that is more precious than the torrents of sunshine the summer dumps upon the beach, and indulging in my melancholy. I
couldn't walk with everyone else because it was difficult talking
about Rebecca's death with people who didn't know her. Or with
people who thought they knew her. I skipped a pebble across the
surface of the ocean like a schoolchild. It made two little skips,
and when it plopped into the ocean with a faintly audible plunk I
felt like an idiot, standing there by myself having some *private
moment with my grief*, that I was standing there alone *staring into
the sea* thinking about my dead friend. She was always going to
die, I thought, sitting in the corner seat of the sofa. We are all
always going to die, but most of us will succumb quietly to an
illness or expire in a nursing home. Rebecca was always going to
*die*. Knowing this made it somehow easier at her funeral to pick

out who knew her and who did not. Those who didn't really know Rebecca were expressing their condolences, were comforting each other, were discussing the cruelty, the randomness, and the horror of her passing. The rest of us turned up at the funeral as if it were an obligation that we'd penciled into our calendars long ago and almost forgotten about, wanted to forget about, some sad but mandatory thing that we knew was coming but we wanted to never have to turn up for, like a root canal or getting a passport renewed. I'd made my way into the diner, where I sat in a corner booth with Emily and with another woman I did not know, but I understood was her girlfriend, even though Nicole had waved me over to join her and Eugene at a rambunctious table full of new young people and Alexander. Alexander was holding forth to the young people about how *Rebecca was one of the greatest undiscovered geniuses of our generation. She was my greatest muse*, he was saying loudly to them. *Though she never made any art of her own, of course, she contributed to the American canon as she was my greatest muse*, he said to the young people, who all nodded solemnly. Actually, she was a great muse. Eugene had once taken a significant photo of Rebecca, in which she was hanging upside down from monkey bars and Eugene had cropped the photo tightly to her upside-down face and flipped it right side up, which sort of made her look confused or constipated, with her upper lip involuntarily curling back to reveal her teeth, her eyebrows artificially raised, and her skin heaving up over her bones. It was clear the photo was of someone beautiful, but it was in no way alluring or even pleasant to look at. The photo was in the collection of a German advertising executive who turned an old Nazi bunker in Berlin into a personal museum for his contemporary art collection, and it rotated in and out of public exhibition every five years. Rebecca never went to Berlin, but she said if she ever did it would have to sync up with when the portrait was in storage. Rebecca! She should have been here now. I couldn't believe I was lunching with Emily and Rebecca wasn't even here. I was glad I had decided to sit with Emily. I clung to Emily and her girlfriend as if they could protect me from the other people I knew. I noticed Nicole was stroking Eugene's arm in the way that I knew from past experience meant Eugene was drunk and itching to make a scene and she was trying to subdue him, and then I overheard as Nicole said to Alexander *it's important to have muses*, I recalled as I sat on the white sofa in Nicole's apartment on the Bowery. *It's important to have muses and we all acted in some way as muses to each other*, she said, and then perhaps responding violently to his partner's imbecilic comment, Eugene wrested his way out from under her straitjacketing and banged on the diner's Formica table and shouted *LET'S HAVE US A LITTLE COFFEE! LET'S GET US SOME COFFEE OVER HERE, WAITRESS*, like a child, and Emily looked at me with great unease. She had never met Eugene and Nicole but likely heard about them from Rebecca, and so she looked at Eugene and then at me as if she were learning something that she did not care to learn about the people her dead friend spent so much time with, that she was getting to know her friend better at this moment. The waitress came to our table and Emily ordered a bacon-lettuce-tomato sandwich and I did the same out of some sense that this would reassure Emily, even though I knew it was a mistake because it was the dead of winter and the tomato would be gray and mealy. She looked tired, she had deeply set circles under her eyes that stuck out especially because it was the sole place where you could see the bone structure, which was recessed especially far back into her soft chubby face. Her black boiler suit set off her short blond hair nicely, but she looked incredibly drawn and tired. She told me she was exhausted from the logistics, that Rebecca's mother had wanted her to have a Catholic funeral in Massachusetts even though she had never been baptized, but that her father, who had become a Richard Dawkins–obsessed doctrinarian atheist, had begged to have her cremated, and even though Rebecca's mother had an iron will and her father was a wimpish man, Rebecca's mother was in possession of a grace and dignity that allowed her to acquiesce. She had said, however, that she couldn't bear to see her beautiful daughter's body turned to soot. She didn't want to touch the ashes or even see the ashes. She wanted nothing to do with the ashes, but at the same time she didn't want her husband to be able to keep whatever remained of their only daughter. To know that Rebecca's final resting place was in some midcentury ceramic urn in his Boston apartment would be almost as if she'd lost some final divorce custody battle, and so Emily, as her oldest friend, took it upon herself the day before the memorial to drive up to Massachusetts and attend to the body, which had been carted away from the third floor of Rebecca's mother's house in a body bag and deposited in a mortuary. Emily had seen them unzip the body bag, which looked a lot like one of those big garment bags she had to carry around the city in her job as a photographer's assistant, and it made her uneasy for a moment, because she was used to unzipping those very same bags and revealing the orange tulle of couture that would be used by her famous photographer boss to dress beautiful women for the covers of fashion magazines, but instead, when the mortician unzipped the bag, inside was her beautiful friend Rebecca, who she had loved and she had followed around the northeast for twenty-odd years, and instead of plucking her from the bag and putting her in front of her boss's camera, which was where of course Rebecca belonged, instead Emily was to arrange for her cremation, a cremation that was shockingly slow—Emily hadn't ever been to a cremation, but she had thought that the body would burn almost instantaneously, but of course it took many hours for the body to become dust. Once it was packed into a box, Rebecca's mother having signed Emily on as *guardian of the ashes*, she drove back to New York to organize the memorial, which merely required she and Rebecca's mother call everyone Rebecca had spoken to her about and have them spread the word that there would be a memorial at the beach in Coney Island. It was all quite automatic, really. Emily hadn't needed to do much thinking because she had actually already spoken about the funeral with Rebecca, *not because Rebecca had planned to die at that very moment*, but because one of Rebecca's favorite things to do was plan imaginary future events—her future wedding, her fortieth birthday party, the celebrations for the opening night of her Tony Award–winning performance—*and so her funeral had been planned years in advance*, Emily said. Of course, it was so like Rebecca that the only event that she had planned to have that actually *occurred* was this funeral. No premiere, no wedding, only a memorial on the beach. And of course this memorial was a fantastic production, and it made me feel sick to imagine how fabulous her wedding party would have been, and how wondrously beautiful she would have been as a bride, to see her statuesque figure in a graceful white, it made me want to weep to think how wonderful, how happy she would have looked on a red carpet, what a spectacle she would have made of herself on a red carpet, how she would have bought ten copies of every tabloid that mentioned whatever ridiculous getup she put together. She was a genius for fashion, I thought. *She was a genius for spectacle*, I said to Emily, *she had an innate sense for spectacle*. The only thing that deviated from Rebecca's funeral plan, which had in fact included her cremation, Emily told me, was the absence of the Chess Player, who hadn't even answered Emily's call or her email. He had moved to Russia last year with his latest girlfriend, an oligarch's daughter who ran a *project space* in Tribeca. Actually, Emily had corrected herself, she was his *wife*. He had married the Russian oligarch's daughter and decamped with her to Moscow, where the game of chess was actually *appreciated*, and even though Rebecca *knew all about the marriage*, because Rebecca had an obsessive habit of tracking his movements through social media—though he naturally didn't use social media, she still managed to find him in the backgrounds of videos his friends posted of parties, she found him referenced in the posts of his chess students' parents. She also discovered that he had moved to Moscow on the Facebook page of the group that organized friendly chess tournaments in the park, which had posted a photo of the goodbye they threw for him at Tompkins Square Park. And even though she knew all this, *even when she was at her absolute lowest*—which from the look that came across Emily's gray, puffy face when she said *lowest* must have been even lower than when I'd seen her last—even at her lowest Rebecca had still harbored hopes that the Chess Player would return. *That absolute creep*, I said, *really ruined her*, and Emily said, well, I don't know if she was ruined, I don't know if he *ruined her*, she never *blamed him* for anything, *she always knew he would return*. I nodded. *Yes*, I said to Emily. *The greatest thing about her was that she lived in a fantasy world*. I wasn't sure if I truly meant this. In fact I had no idea what I meant by this. I'd actually despised Rebecca's insistence on breaking so thoroughly with reality at every opportunity, and then I noticed Eugene was drunkenly wobbling. In his stupor he had been snatching up the toothpicks from the sandwiches of everyone at his table and inserting them into one end of his straw and blowing them out the other, shooting the toothpicks up at the foam ceiling, where they stuck, their little colored cellophane flags sticking down as if Eugene were planting his colonial claim on the roof, and I felt angry at Rebecca for dying, I felt really angry with her for killing herself because in a sense, Rebecca had been dead to me for about five years. I heard nothing from her and rarely, if ever, thought about her, and so by actually dying, by *really* dying, it was all her fault that I had come here. It was all her fault, I thought as I sat on the sofa, that I was here now in the apartment on the Bowery. It was her fault that when her mother called me two days ago to tell me she was dead, to make sense of my state of shock I had to go pace up and down the Bowery like a madwoman, and so it was all Rebecca's fault that I had ended up outside the café, that I had run into Eugene in a state of shock, a state of shock that *she had put me in with her selfishness*, and that I had accepted the invitation to this little dinner on the Bowery, full of the people that I had made every effort to avoid, each and every one of them a totally disgusting person who I had known for years, people who were New York's most famous and well-regarded artists, failures all. I looked across the room at an independent film producer who used his tie-dye clothing and *chill vibes* to distract from his widely known sexual predation. Missing from the scene was the *up-and-coming* director whose next film he was financing, a man who had once been a frequent guest at Nicole and Eugene's but tonight was *on location* and wouldn't be able to make it. The director was a slight, boyish thirty-something who always wore a grimy gray baseball cap with the team logo fraying even when he was in a suit at a gala or a film festival. He always tried to look out of place at events that signified his *arrival*, I guess as a way of sending a message that he hadn't *bought into* the world he'd entered since the runaway success of his last film, a surprise likely even to him, as it wasn't much different from his others, which featured the same shaky camerawork and gratuitous sex scenes and *meaningful* sequences of tracking shots set to vintage disco music. The producer was explaining the conceit of the film he was to make with the up-and-coming director and the actress we were all still waiting for to arrive. It was based on a French novel, the title of which he was struggling to remember. Alexander interrupted him to ask if he knew of a certain film production company, the name of which even I knew, as it was one of the world's largest. *Is it any good?* Alexander asked the film producer. The producer said that it was probably the only company he would work for besides his own, but that he'd never work anywhere with offices and name tags and HR personnel, which made sense to me because then he would probably wind up in prison. *I like a more gritty, authentic style*, the film producer said. I knew that Alexander's novel was bought by the production company, and he was desperate to tell this to the producer, but he left no opening for Alexander to do so. Meanwhile, I was annoyed that from half listening to the conversation taking place around me I was now up to date on the cultural production of downtown New York, that through being here I had overheard that the actress we were waiting for *had signed on to play the lead* in the new movie because she was *a huge fan of the raw vibe of the last one* and had actually *had her agents reach out* to *take a meeting* with the film director, which *completely shocked* the director but actually *made total sense to him* because it's the kind of thing *anyone interested in holding a mirror up to our corrupt relationship to the image would understand.* Yes, the room at Eugene and Nicole's was full of New York's most famous and well-regarded artists, who were failures, just as Eugene and Nicole were failures. They had wildly successful careers and yet they were complete artistic failures and it made me feel sick with regret, sick with embarrassment, that when I had first been an adult in New York I had held these people in such high esteem. The liberal careerist world of my childhood was what I thought I was escaping by becoming friends with these artists, but in fact they were the very same as those liberal careerists, sometimes even worse. They were even more conservative, even more classist, more cowardly, stupider. They were interested in the same kind of aesthetic of legibility, of "correctness," not as *political correctness* but as *I checked off all the boxes, I did what I was meant to do, I made a piece of art that can be understood as art*, they were successful according to the very same rubric that they would know to call *neoliberal* in a derisive tone but was the exact rubric of neoliberal achievement they too followed. They wanted money, fame, and power, and used art only as a means to these ends, and the desire they had to *shock the liberals* was merely the new language *of* liberal careerism. I knew they wanted to use their platforms to tell people just how stupid they were for buying hybrid cars, how hopelessly middle class they were for caring about politics, they wanted to critique the feminism of mainstream celebrities, accuse people of brainless consumerism, make fun of people for being fat, for being ugly, they wanted to shock the mainstream with all of their fringe opinions, all while trying to generate buzz about themselves in the hopes of getting to direct a fashion ad or produce a

Hollywood film. The ideas and aesthetics of the avant-garde, the bohemian scenes, the experimental musicians, have of course always fed the mainstream culture, but, I felt, as I sat in my corner seat on the sofa, never was *the lifestyle of the bohemian* so clearly *the product that was being sold* in an attempt to *enter the mainstream.* The bohemian life was always of interest to the majority culture, but it was because the people within it had something to say—there was something going on *within* their universe that the mainstream wanted access to. It wasn't a matter of selling out. It was that there was nothing to sell. The actress who was to be our *guest of honor* had in particular made a persona of sharing her lifestyle and opinions with the world. The films she made, I thought, were merely the *smallest thing she could do* to have an article written about her. All that was important to her was to have the article written about her, to win the award, to have the interview. Or at least that's what it seemed like to me, given that I'd seen these films and it would be worse to actually want to be *known* for putting such dreck into the world than for being a *successful actress.* Andy Warhol stole everything from the people that wanted to be around him and his artistic fame, he stole all of their thoughts, all of their stories and ideas, and put them into his films. He recorded them as they spoke and he used the recordings in his films and his books. Their lifestyle was important so that Andy could make his art and it all fed into itself. Most of the hippies became boring as boomers, but at least they were having a good time together and not desperately trying to make Hollywood films loosely based on their lives while they were on acid in Haight-Ashbury. I don't mean to fetishize *living in the moment*, but it seemed to me like Eugene, Nicole, the actress, were all *living to prove that they had lived*. And this, most of all, more than their unlived-in houses and their unread books and their unused minds, was why I despised Eugene and Nicole and these idiots I had managed to take a vacation from until tonight. Because they had enticed me with the promise of an artistic community and made me believe when I was nineteen that their world was a wonderful place where people exchanged ideas and created things together, for a public, for each other, with a purpose. I had believed them, and I thought that when they were cruel to others it was for the greater benefit of the higher ideal that was art. When they excluded someone purposefully from a dinner party, when they laughed in someone's face, when they made a display of hating their art—like the time that Nicole got so drunk at an opening she told the painter's husband, pretending not to know who he was, that the show was absolute bourgeois garbage—they made me believe that these cruelties were necessary to uphold the sanctity of something greater, of art, and because I am of a weak will and of a simpering and pathetic character, I allowed myself to be influenced by them. I became known as a judgmental person. I was cruel to people, and though I was often a good judge of who deserved poor treatment, I also behaved badly toward people who were simply weaker than I was, otherwise benign people who lacked the mental faculties to produce good work, to produce good conversation, because being cruel is easy, it is fun, it is seductive, especially if you enjoy conversation and have a quick tongue, which I do. I always know just what to say to give someone a dressing-down, and I loved it when Nicole laughed when I said the right thing, disarming someone she hated, even if they probably didn't deserve cruel treatment, because I am a total weakling lacking in character, and so I could never forgive Nicole and Eugene, because I could never forgive myself for abandoning myself, for making myself believe that I was not the tender and soft girl who had sewn bunny rabbit dolls from socks for my third-grade teacher, who had sung along to folk songs about plants and freedom and labor organizing in the car with my grandfather, but instead that I was a vicious attack dog. I had let them harness my intelligence and my quick wit as a weapon. I had led myself to believe that I had to choose between the didactic and humorless world of politics and the soulless and cruel world of art, and it made me feel completely sick to know that I'd once thought I had finally found people from whom I could learn something about art, and I started laughing to myself in my seat on the corner of the sofa, laughing hard to myself out loud, repeating *learn something about art* out loud to myself, at first under my breath but then loud enough for the people around to hear me as I repeated, *learn something about art*, and I saw them all look at me, confused by what I was saying to myself, by the unseemly display I was making there on the sofa. Or perhaps they were confused to see me here at all, because though I was treating this dinner as if it were a reunion of people who had long since *fallen out*, as if everyone in attendance should feel *out of place in their old stomping grounds*, this was actually a normal evening in the course of their usual lives. I noticed that one of the people who was looking at me was Clara Carson, a beautiful brunette a few years older than me who still dressed like a tarty goth teenager at a suburban mall—Clara who one could call an artist if one stretched the definition of art so wide as to include the *multimedia sculptural fairyland bullshit dioramas* she made, Clara who had been hanging around Eugene and Nicole for as long as I had, was here seeming in perfect harmony with her surroundings. I couldn't believe that these people were *still* always at the Bowery, these great successful artists, artistic failures all, that they were all still best friends with one another. When I left I hadn't even thought that it was possible that it still existed, not because my departure could have created some kind of vacuum that forced the *scene* to *collapse in on itself*, but because it simply hadn't entered my mind that there was an enduring link between any of these people. But clearly, as I looked around and saw Clara Carson *still* purposefully wearing a dress so low-cut and flimsy that her small breasts were exposed every time she leaned slightly forward, and watched Alexander and Eugene *still* sneaking furtive glances at her nipples every time this happened, it appeared that nothing really had changed. There were of course new people, like the young artist that Eugene had been pawing at all night, a woman in her early twenties with a round face packed with exaggerated yet balanced, lovely features. On top of this face she had frizzled curls that were bleached and dyed an unfortunate shade of copper, which for some reason has always been one of my least favorite ways for a person to look.

Bleached curly hair. It's tragic to me not only because the bleached curly hair looks so fried but because nothing looks more beautiful than luscious curly hair. Looking bad is not a moral failing if it's the only option available to you. But by reading the misguided hair choices you can see the similarly misguided trend-following nature of the brain beneath. The young artist's hair, as much as the way she had at one point been sitting on Eugene's lap, made me understand that she was capable of making very bad choices in life as in her appearance. She had been ensnared by the loft on the Bowery, among the others who, unlike me, had not escaped. They had remained in New York under the thumb of Eugene and Nicole, and under their tutelage, and *with their permission* they had become successful artists in New York. They had solo shows at blue-chip galleries that Eugene often arranged for them with his gallery, with his father's connections, and Nicole arranged for their work to be collected by major museums in New York and in Dubai and in Los Angeles and in Vienna and even in London, where I often came across it, the work that was just as awful as I remembered, just as facile, just as *art-like* and just as *artless* as it had been when I had known them in New York. And when I had seen them all at the funeral this came into even clearer focus for me: that these people all thought they were the great intellectuals of their time, that they had read the curriculum vitae of the previous generation of cultural avant-garde as a map plan for membership, that this cultural avant-garde had decided that the criteria for the membership was a sufficient number of exhibitions in Chelsea with big gallery dinners to follow. All they needed to see to was that their film premiered at the Venice Biennale to a packed room of actors in black tie. If they were asked to creative direct an advertisement for the *most avant-garde fashion house*, that, even, would be sufficient for membership. And yet all their work was hopelessly banal, all their work was cooked up in a nervous frenzy because they'd spent all their mental energy maneuvering to get a show at the right gallery. The films were incredibly boring because so much time was spent securing backers for their next project, the art was made in a slapdash fashion in order only to fill the necessary space before the gallery dinner, to fill the space before the party in Cannes, and so Eugene's works, and the works of others in the room that I could see from my perch on the white sofa, the work of Clara Carson, who I could see talking to Nicole, for example, contained the simplest ideas that weren't even elegant in their simplicity, weren't even daringly, poignantly simple. They were obvious and legible, they were *ideas*, Clara made things like *sculptures* that were just old models of iPhones encased in resin, she made work that said *this is what I think about technology*. They all made work like this. Sometimes it was *this is what I think about my ancestors*, or *this is what I think about climate change*, or even *this is what I think about the concept of indigeneity*, which was incredibly easy for curators like Nicole to understand and so incredibly attractive since curators of course can only understand things that are incredibly easy to understand, and so Eugene and the rest hardly ever had a *break* between gallery shows, and the curators typed up their wall texts and slapped them up beside whatever boring bricolage was on view. *This piece interrogates notions of whateverthehell.* I remember going to one of Clara Carson's exhibitions that Nicole had organized on one floor of the New Museum, and it was written up as a *blockbuster show of contemporary art,* and the show really was packed, and I noticed that the public would read the wall text before looking at the piece. They'd enter the gallery and look directly at the wall text and then they'd cast a passing glance at the piece itself—and who could blame them, I mean the pieces were hardly visually interesting, they were hardly arresting, they were hardly even beautiful—and then, having read the wall text they'd think *I understand the piece completely,* they'd nod their head, *ah yes, this reptile terrarium filled with mercury is of course about the contamination of our oceans, as I've just learned on the wall text,* and they'd check off a mental box, the artist had done what she'd promised, and they'd move on to the next one and do the same, and they'd leave the room feeling like they had gone and seen some culture that they had really understood for once, they'd understood the point the artist was trying to make because it was right there to read on the wall text, and of course it made sense. It was an idea, an idea about a world problem, about the artist's identity, and why couldn't everything be like this, they thought—why did the things they saw in the modern art museum have to make such little sense? What on earth was that Rauschenberg guy getting at painting his canvases white? I mean what on earth was that toilet bowl doing sitting there in an art museum, and those sculptures that are just rocks, just plain rocks, well, what is it that those rocks are about? They didn't have to have these kinds of thoughts in the contemporary art wing, at the shows that Nicole curated. Nicole once curated a museum exhibition where her cronies' contemporary art was hung next to old master portraiture in order to show the stark contrast between the contemporary and the classic. It has to be said, Nicole is a genius for that. Nicole is absolutely brilliant for this idea, because if these pieces were shown next to any piece made after the year 1950, anyone with two brain cells to rub together would be able to see just how little progress has been made in art and the general public would revolt against the art museum, I mean they would take up arms against the collection of pennies that calls itself the National Endowment for the Arts, and they would have every right. They would demand *that some progress be made with their tax dollars.* There was an artist, Simon, who Eugene and Nicole collected, a painter, whose works were in the show, and in fact one of his paintings was in this very room, I noticed as I sat on the white sofa. His paintings were done in the style of old master portraits, but the models were holding contemporary objects. Instead of a milkmaid holding a jug of milk, a model with a fashionable mullet haircut was holding a carton of oat milk and wearing orange Crocs sandals. In one painting, commissioned by Dior, the sitter wore head-to-toe Dior couture. Now, this must have been a difficult show for Nicole to write a wall text for, because even though this artist's paintings sold like crazy, what on earth was the artist doing—what was his idea? The painter had made no aesthetic progress since the old master paintings that hung beside his, and there was no conceptual idea, really, beyond *we now have different things than before*, which was how Nicole managed to frame the show as *a commentary on humor and consumerism*. Except of course these paintings were churned out for the market, and of course, the only commentary the painter was making on consumerism was that he loved it, and the only humor involved was the twisted joke that his paintings should be shown next to a Rembrandt. And yet this painter is of course at the center of New York's avant-garde, this painter is the exact synecdochical embodiment of New York's avant-garde. What had this painter done that was genuinely avant-garde? I mean, without question this contemporary avant-garde is descended from the modernist avant-garde of almost one hundred years ago—an avant-garde that was quite radical, that was even *hostile* to the general public—and what this artist and his milieu stand for neuters, no, spits on the radical notions of postmodernism, of the rejection of form, of the rejection of the audience, of the desire to *make the audience suffer*, and instead they repurpose the aesthetics to transpose them into a palatable and popular form. So of course Nicole had to pair Simon's paintings with the old masters. If these works were shown next to Picasso's, or even next to Hockney's, the entire ruse, the historical reenactment photo-booth style of Simon's novelty portraiture would be exposed. It was the fault of Nicole and her ilk for rewarding their behavior, for validating their projects, I thought, as I looked at one of Simon's portraits that was hung across from my seat on the white sofa, a sort of

brownish-orange number, very paintstroke-y, of a fashion-
model-slash-florist painted in the same serio-grotesque style as
the ikebana arrangements she made out of fine flowers, drift-
wood, and her own garbage. It was one of Simon's earlier paintings, before he really figured out how to do eyes properly, so the
model had a bit of a tropical-lizard look to her bulging eyes. The
most skillful part of the painting was the way Simon had rendered the model's trash, a bricolage of makeup packaging, innovative seltzers, and crumpled-up moist towelettes. I was staring
at a painting of trash. The people in this room on the Bowery, at
this dinner party, made up of *New York's most successful artists*,
fancied themselves to be great intellectuals for the sole reason
that New York embraced them, believing that they had passed
some kind of aesthetic and intellectual test beyond the fact that
the galleries of New York had embraced them. It depressed me
deeply to think that Rebecca had forced me through her death to
resume my association with these people, her friends, and when
I recalled that she still associated with them up until her death, I
thought that the Chess Player was right to call her apartment the
skittles room, the room where nothing mattered, the room where
noncompetitors played scrimmage matches against other nonentities who weren't in it for real, because that was who Rebecca
associated with. It really was the skittles room. And then I felt
disgusted with myself, suddenly, recalling the way that I had behaved when the chess master left Rebecca, the way I had abandoned her. I had given up my friendship with her without a
second thought. I remembered sitting at the diner with Emily,

hearing Emily tell me about Rebecca's two stints at a rehab facility in upstate New York, one of which was paid for by her father,
who reluctantly dipped into what he'd called his meager savings
that he'd been accumulating since his *financial ruin*, forestalling
his trip to Hawaii with the tennis partner, and how, when Rebecca returned, she found two new psychiatrists who were willing to prescribe her benzodiazepines and began taking one
prescription to the CVS and the other prescription to her usual
Duane Reade to double the dose. And then, Emily told me, she
had found a twenty-something-year-old skateboarder through a
dating app who had become her lover and knew how to order
opioids using Bitcoin, and that's when her problem got even
worse. Emily would come home from long stints upstate for pho-
toshoots to find her passed out on the floor naked, and eventually
Emily's boss had helped Rebecca to go to a *second* rehab, run by
a pseudo-religious cult, which was free but also didn't take because it mostly relied on saunas and vitamins and praying to
aliens, and when she was released she came back to the city, re-
stocked her pharmaceuticals, and took a Greyhound bus up to
the Cape. This was about two months ago, which I realized was
right around the time that I'd returned from London without
telling anyone, and I thought, as I sat on the sofa, that had I not
abandoned Rebecca, had I not condemned her for her weakness,
she might have been here at the Bowery tonight instead of me,
and then I had to stop thinking about the hypotheticals. Instead
I thought about the despicable way that I had behaved at the funeral, the way that I had stood watching Alexander give his

poem, my arms crossed in disapproval, not only because his poem was the effluviant rambling of a tasteless egomaniac, but also because I was behaving as though I was the one who was Rebecca's very best friend. I had appointed myself to safeguard the attention that she was owed at the funeral, and remembering this I was disgusted by the knowing look that I had given to Emily when she passed out the ashes, as if to say that she and I were the only ones that knew each other's pain, that we were the closest to Rebecca. I was humiliated, I thought, sitting on the sofa, by the way I was overcome with rage in the Coney Island diner when I heard Nicole tell the people about the dinner they were throwing for the actress, that I had thought it was *my* role to safeguard the propriety of the funeral, to ensure Rebecca's memory was being honored. Most of all, I realized as I sat on the white sofa, I was horrified that I had sat with Emily and her girl-friend at the diner, that I had monopolized Emily, that I had considered my friendship with Rebecca's to be on a par with Emily's—Rebecca, who I hadn't heard from in years, who, the last time I had seen her, had told me I had abandoned her. I knew, as I sat on the white sofa, that it was ridiculous, I knew that it was really she who had abandoned me for the Chess Player when I had loved her so deeply, but at the same time I also knew that I had abandoned her when she needed my strength. I had held her to the standard of someone much stronger than she was. I had left her that day in her apartment, alone with her histrionics, and I had thought, well, of course Emily, wherever she is, can deal with this, but I had known that she couldn't. At the diner it became abundantly clear to me that this was not a person who in any way had *control* over anybody—and I had known that from the start, from the way that Emily had wanted to be an artist but had never dared accompany Rebecca to any parties, the way she was too afraid to meet people that she looked up to, the way that Rebecca had completely dominated Emily, had completely stunned her since childhood. I had made myself believe, in pure fancy, that Emily could have rescued her. I realized as I sat on the white sofa that I had no idea what Rebecca had really been going through. I had always assumed she was using her drug problem for attention, she was using it as a crutch to explain away her unsuccessful artistic career, and that because of the way she was able to project control over the drug use, because she was able to turn her mental problems into an exaggerated performance, which I should have been able to see through but it was more convenient to believe, I had no sympathy for her mental problems because I did not like how she expressed them. I had no sympathy for her suffering, and in fact I had used her. I had used her suffering, I had used her charisma, I had used her life story, her magnetism, to launch my own successful career in the arts because she was the first person to show me that with the right encouragement I could make something that other people were really interested in. I had allowed her to die, I thought, sitting on the white sofa, and just as I was about to begin crying, just as I was about to rouse myself from the seat on the white sofa and leave without uttering a word to any of the vultures here on the Bowery I felt Nicole's hand on my shoulder, or rather I felt *some* hand on my shoulder and *smelled* Nicole's vetiver oil and made an *educated guess* that the hand belonged to Nicole, and a voice—definitely Nicole's: *low, sensual, disgusting*—told me that the actress had arrived some minutes ago and that dinner was to be served. I looked up and saw that everyone had gotten up and moved to the table, a long piece of live-edged wood propped up by sawhorses, and that the actress's arrival had gone unnoticed while I had my eyes closed thinking about Rebecca. Everyone must have gotten up from their seats around me in the living room and moved to the table, where I could see them all sitting now, acting as if they didn't notice that I was still sitting on the sofa in what I'm sure they thought was a supreme display of generosity—their pretending that they did not notice me with my eyes closed on my seat at the sofa—and now they had sent Nicole to tell me they were waiting for me to take my seat at the table. Under any other circumstance I would have felt embarrassed by this, by the idea that I had drifted off publicly, but I felt as though I had already degraded myself by showing up to this apartment on the Bowery that nothing could top the embarrassment of assenting to sit in the same room as these people. I mean, I had already made a big show of excommunicating myself from this world only to allow myself to be sucked back in at the very first opportunity, and so it was clear that shamelessness was my only mode of engagement, and in fact, my falling asleep was the only thing that saved me from this shamelessness. Sleeping displayed my lack of interest in being at the party at all, so actually I felt pleased with myself. I had sobered up during my nap and so

I sprang up from my seat on the sofa, which startled Nicole, she was literally *taken aback*, and then when she regained her composure I followed my hostess to the table, where I finally saw the actress, at long last, installed in an honorific position at the center of the table. Eugene had completely monopolized her, drawing her in closely for an *intimate conversation* before anyone else could speak to her, but from what I could see she was more unassuming than I'd imagined and it seemed ridiculous that we'd all been waiting for *this person* so that we could have dinner, that I'd spent hours suffering and starving on the sofa for this petite specimen who wasn't even volunteering a mea culpa for making us wait, though perhaps I had missed it while I was asleep. Nicole led me to a seat near the edge of the table, where, naturally, I was seated across from Alexander, who had behaved so terribly at the funeral in Coney Island that just looking at him made me sneer. Nicole must have done this on purpose, I thought, she sat us together to spite me, which was confirmed when she said *this will give you two time to catch up*, and smiled at me with a variation on her trademark wince-smile. Nicole really had once been a beautiful woman, I thought, looking at her slightly altered wince-smile. Nicole had once been the most glamorous person I had ever met. She wore no makeup and had the creamiest-looking skin—it wasn't just moisturized, it was creamy—and she was always wearing the most beautifully draped clothing, things that looked so plain, with no discernible designer, that looked heartbreakingly expensive, but in these past five years something had happened to her face, a thing I now realized was

Botox, which had stripped her facial musculature of its ability to produce withering looks, and instead made her look simply dumb. I had been wondering why she looked so *dumb* at Rebecca's funeral, why she seemed so incredibly *emotionless*, so incredibly *dumb* at Coney Island, and I realized, as she attempted to make a look that must have signified, *I've put you here with Alexander to ensure you will suffer*, which of course I was doing without her intervention, I realized as she turned to me with a sort of trapped-behind-the-eyes look of those who have suffered a tragic accident that rendered them a *vegetable*, I realized that she had paralyzed her face into *dumbness*. And so I replied to her attempt to make this face at me with a wild smile of my own, with a smile that used every muscle available to me, which is very many more than the average person—I've always had an incredibly expressive face, so much so that my inability to control it has gotten me into trouble in both my professional and social lives. I smiled a great impudent smile at Nicole, and she looked at me, her eyes locked behind that inflexible canvas, and she told the hired caterer who was standing by the door to the kitchen that the soup could be served. I hoped that the soup would be Nicole's watercress soup, which I actually loved, but I knew that I would be unable to enjoy whatever Nicole served for dinner because being seated across from Alexander nauseated me. I realized I had been unfair to Rebecca earlier, as I sat across from Alexander. I realized it was not Rebecca's fault that I had returned here to the Bowery at all. It was Alexander's fault. Unequivocally it was Alexander's fault that I had come here at all. It was Alexander who had scooped me up *from obscurity* and dragged me to the loft on the Bowery after I returned to New York from my short stint at college in Ohio, where I had been inundated with *theory*, inundated with people obsessed by *art* and by *theory*. I had returned to New York having sworn off artists, having sworn off *theory* and Alexander had snatched me up in his talons and deposited me right back in these people's nest. In college I had refused to interact with people my age who called themselves *artists*—it humiliated me really, the way they desired the title more than they had any interest in *the production of art*—but the people I really refused to associate with were the people that called themselves *writers*, the people who said *I am a writer*, as if their diaries contained anything more than the usual pathetic longing and suicidal thoughts of the teenaged fools that voluntarily call themselves *writers*, the cringing introverts that call themselves *writers*. Even though I, myself, had always intended to write, I would never dare to call myself *a writer*. What a humiliating way to identify yourself. *A writer.* You may as well say I am a *pooper*, I am a *pisser*. I would never dare call myself an *artist* the way these people I met in college did. It terrified me the way that no one had any *real interest in literature*, the way the creative writing students, the *writers*, read nothing but drafts of each other's short stories about cheating on their girlfriends, and the *English major* was merely a refuge for the intellectually incurious, for those without the rigor to learn a language or the drive to challenge themselves to master a science or skill. I attended a few literature classes but found that many of the people in the seminars *had not read the novels that we were assigned*—that they were *proud of this fact*, that after class they'd brag to one another about having *not completed the reading*, and that they'd speak their opinions about the text freely during the seminar, they'd craft some opinion about the Victorian novel that they *had not read* by skimming some criticism. I remember one particular student aping the opinion of a critic who wrote a personal essay about her experience of rereading *Middlemarch* yearly and what that meant for her, which I had also read because it was the sort of thing that my mother sent me that I liked to read while using the facilities. But I had read the magazine piece in addition to actually reading the book *Middlemarch*, and so when the student aped the opinions of the article's author I was prepared for the professor to intervene and expose the student's laziness, but instead of standing up to the student, instead of dressing the student down for not having read the book at all, the professor nodded and spoke at length about also having read the piece in the *New Yorker*, praising the piece, praising the *New Yorker*, praising the student for reading the *New Yorker* as if subscribing to this middlebrow magazine was equivalent to translating the Rosetta stone in your free time, and then we were stuck discussing the professor's own history of attempting to get a similar style of piece published by the *New Yorker*, alas to no avail. At this high-level literature seminar at a prestigious institution of higher education *Middlemarch* was probably discussed for thirty minutes, and by people who had in large part not read it, and I was heartbroken, though not surprised, that people who had come to a so-called *temple of higher education* to study literature *did not want to speak to me about books*. I was infuriated that the professors who had secured *jobs for life* in order to *safeguard the canon, problematize the canon, deconstruct the canon*, or do whatever it was they wanted to do with the canon were so afraid of *censuring their students* that all they were able to do was *placate them* and *congratulate them* for doing the absolute minimum. And so I left the English department, as I knew that I did not need to devote my education to reading literature alongside people who were interested in merely learning how to yada yada their way through a conversation about books that I could read—or, of course, not read—on my own. Socially, for the short period I was in college, I did go to parties with the so-called *artists*, because they had a real talent for whisking together something fun, they had a real talent for procuring alcohol underage, for securing an empty building for a party, for getting things together. They had the ingenuity of great artists in that way, and so I did associate with the *artistic set* even then, but I tired of their conversations about *cybernetics theory* that were really about *networking with gallerists*, about *futurism* that were really about *ambition*, and so when I returned to New York I swore off the *artistic life*. I swore off the people who were *interested in theory*, and I lived in a world devoid of anything that so much as *resembled* these people. I lived in a world free of interesting-looking sneakers and rimless eyeglasses and meaningfully cuffed trousers. I went only to the Met and the Guggenheim and the Frick, sometimes MoMA, and only on the weekends, when I could be sure that the place would be packed full of tourists and families with young children. I didn't dare enter those museums on the weekdays during daylight hours, when only the artists and the elderly and the unemployed could visit. I had no problem with the elderly or the unemployed—in fact I believed that all the funding that galleries and collectors and private foundations doled out to these young artists that I met in university for their projects *interrogating* whatever it was that they would *instrumentalize* for their career successes should be expropriated and handed out among the unemployed and the elderly, that the various artistic foundations should empty their bank accounts into the trust of the Social Security Administration—but I managed to maintain my distance from the *artistic world* while seeing the treasures of the museums, the Italian busts, the antique baseball cards in the basement of the American Wing at the Met, their ancient everyday artifacts, the terra-cotta bowls, the Egyptian beads. My favorite were the ancient Roman glass objects, and I loved that I was able to walk through the museum and find the moment in time when vessels went from being solely opaque entities, solely solid objects, and became translucent. I couldn't imagine what it was like to drink from your first glass cup, see the light dancing on the water you were about to drink after a life of holding water only in ceramicized mud. I stood there at the Met looking at this ancient Roman glass drinking cup thinking about how it is absolutely mad that people believe that because of *modern technology* we are living in the greatest period for innovation, because you can order dishwashing liquid by telling an inanimate object to order it for you, when thousands of years ago, suddenly the opaque became transparent, and while I had been having these stupid, self-important thoughts about the discovery of glass, I was approached by a tall, admittedly handsome stranger, who I now sat across from at the table at Eugene's, the tall and handsome stranger who had become the ugly and familiar Alexander, who found the need to approach me at the Met and tell me that my shoelace was untied. I should have known then and there to run for the hills. It is only the worst people in the world who tell you that your shoelace is untied, the most intrusive, condescending people who let you know that your shoelace is untied. They have some kind of perverse desire to invade your personal space to inform you that you've been incapable of doing the simplest thing, and they alert you as though they are truly worried for your personal safety—that by leaving your shoe untied you are opening yourself up to the most severe bodily harm, and that they, by warning you of something that doubtlessly you're able to see, are absolute saints of the highest order, when in reality you've left your shoe untied because once it's dragged around on the dirty floor for long enough, you're well aware it's come undone but why on earth would you want to touch the muddy shoelace and tie it, and Alexander pointed at my shoelace, and as I was about to tell him that I knew my shoelace was untied, I looked down and noticed his shoelace was untied too, and my face of approbation softened into a smile. That was how I became friends with Alexander, and how I got to know Eugene, and Nicole, and got dragged back into the artistic world that I had disavowed when I left college. Ten years later I watched as a bowl of soup was placed in front of his stupid face. The soup was brown and, as was standard at the dinners on the Bowery, made from some kind of outré vegetable; this time it was sunchoke, its surface mottled with olive oil. Alexander scraped his spoon on the bottom of the bowl, even though it was totally full, as if he was determined to have bad table manners in some kind of show of exaggerated indelicacy to prove that he was *tougher*, that he was *grittier* than these soft, spoiled people that he associated with. Alexander was the son of a doctor. He had gone to private university, had no student debt, and spent summertime visiting beachfront properties owned by members of his family, but because his family's upper-middle-class position didn't allow him access to the unlimited wealth that other people who had chosen *artistic careers* enjoyed, in his mind he was destitute. On the rare occasions he went to restaurants he ordered the cheapest thing on the menu—I had even seen him order a single boiled egg at a French restaurant—and he always made a show of making sure the waiter understood he'd asked for tap water. He used to put his drinks at bars on other people's tabs, proudly, in a way that to me, at first, seemed like a playful joke *taking advantage of the rich*, but then on further inspection seemed pathetic, completely pathetic, to be a grown man stealing four-dollar beers from strangers. Unlike people who are actually broke, who tend to hide the fact that they cannot afford things because of the shame attached to it, unlike, say, Rebecca, who really needed people to buy drinks for her because she often had zero dollars in her bank

account, though she would never say that, Alexander wanted
you to know that he had nothing. In his mind he was like Patti
Smith showing up in New York City with a backpack and twenty
dollars she found on the ground in the bus terminal. In reality,
when Alexander arrived in New York, he was deposited in the
safe confines of an NYU dorm room by both of his parents. And,
though Alexander's parents did not buy him a large loft on the
Bowery, or even pay his rent, they paid for the furniture and security deposit. Years later they gave him their Toyota when they
got a new one, and the novel that propelled him into *literary stardom* was written with support from his grandmother, who died
leaving him fifty thousand dollars, allowing him to quit his job
at a bookstore and focus completely on writing fiction. This fifty
thousand dollars only made him even worse when it came to
money. It was as if he thought this fifty thousand dollars was the
only money he would ever have in his entire life and he needed
to make it last until his Social Security benefits kicked in at sixty-
five. I appreciated that any money he had was funneled into life
preservation in order not to have to go back to working, and
thereby taking time away from writing his novel, but even with
the large endowment from his relative, he was still glum, mi-
serly, and bitter about money. His imagined destitution gave him
permission to criticize everyone for the smallest things that
soften life's edges. To him, a meal at a nice restaurant was useless
unless someone else was paying. A new pair of shoes was a moral
failing. When he was invited on a short trip to Mexico, even
though the villa was paid for by Eugene, he considered it to be a

decadence he could not imagine partaking in. Pathetically, I thought as I sat on my corner seat of the sofa, I can now see that Alexander's hysterical attitude about money was actually the behavior of someone quite spoiled who believed he deserved more. But at that time Alexander was so domineering, his voice so whiny and loud, his tone so declarative, I could not help but understand his stance on money, on self-abnegation, as being *the truth*. When a magazine paid for me to review a luxury hotel in Miami, I knew I couldn't tell Alexander or else he would think that I was frivolous, and then when I did tell him, because of course I am frivolous and I couldn't help myself, he replied that *it must be nice to be so rich*, that it *must be nice* to be able to afford things like that, even though I had said that it was paid for, but he said that I was *rich in another currency*, he said that I was *paying for it in a different way*, which of course I agreed with. He said that *dealing in that currency was worse than traditional capital*—he was often using the word *capital* in that era because he was seeing a girl who worked for a left-wing magazine and was trying his hardest to pretend that he knew about anything besides contemporary American literature—and even though I knew *dealing in that currency* was *not* worse than *in capital*, I began to feel sorry for myself. I began to feel like I was a frivolous person, like I could easily be bought by the public relations firm that paid for my business-class ticket and luxury suite in Miami, that the price of my soul was two nights watching television and ordering room service in the nicest hotel room I'd ever slept in, that I was an idiot for desiring creature comforts, that I wrote nice things about the hotel because I was paid to, and so not only could my body be bought but my mind could as well. I was disgusted with myself until I remembered that Alexander had gone on a trip to France with his family, with his brother and with their parents, who paid for everything, and they had stayed at luxurious hotels and visited vineyards, and Alexander had talked about it to me not as if he had been invited on a nice family holiday paid for by his parents, and therefore by his connections to them, but like his week luxuriating in the Loire Valley was something he had *stolen* from these *rich people* who, suddenly, he had nothing to do with, as if he had like a cunning trickster *lucked his way* into a beautiful time sampling white wines and visiting châteaus, as if he had *scrounged until then*. But even still, even though I knew about the trip he had taken, Alexander made me feel guilty, and I adopted a guilty detached affect. I acted like *I* felt guilty, or really, because I am a worm, I *actually felt* guilty, when I told him about my trip to Miami, like I wasn't ever going to become a real writer or a real artist or someone worthy of respect because I allowed myself to trade my talent, meager that it was, for finery that only vulgar people could ever want. Had I traded my meager talent for something like free hardback novels to review, then maybe I could have won Alexander's approval, but because I was interested in luxury I wasn't really an artist. In this regard, I have always been incredibly weak. I allow the shoddy moral frameworks of people I hardly respect to influence how I feel. If there is a single shred of truth to their accusations, suddenly my paranoiac tendencies are stoked and fed by my own ambivalent feelings toward myself. I have always allowed people to get the best of me in this way. By giving them credit for my own conflicting thoughts, I cast myself as the worst version of myself because that's what they want me to do. This, in earlier times, would cause me to rebel in the most idiotic way, in the very way that Alexander rebels against the wealthy, punishing them because he is not one of them. In fact Alexander had influenced me in this way many times. He had influenced me to behave in that same strange, peevish, rude way around wealthy people, that same demonstrably superior way that he affects, where he'll open a bottle of wine from their kitchen without asking, and say within earshot *it doesn't matter to them*, which, though it's probably true, does nothing but make Alexander look like an ass, an ungracious ass who is unlikely to be invited back to drink the *free wine*, which, of course, as from my seat at the dining room table on the Bowery, at Eugene's house, drinking his wine and speaking to no one, I related to. I relate to this feeling of ungraciousness, and actually I support it, but when Alexander behaves like that he seems worse than an ingrate—he looks pathetic, he looks hungry, he looks as if he is desperate for comfort, which is of course the easiest way to be denied comfort, by looking starved for it. Rebecca, I thought, was the worst off of all of us, though she never appeared so, because the moment she had any money she would spend it on you as if she were rich, or dying, I thought, glancing back at the facsimile of Rebecca's red blanket in the other room. Rebecca had bought me dinner on more occasions than I could remember, just because she'd recently been paid.

When Rebecca had a job hanging up people's coats at the downtown French restaurant where Nicole and Eugene had a reserved
table, where Nicole and Eugene's photographs hung on the wall,
their bloated faces smiling next to the owner's, she made enough
money to pay her rent in a few nights, and after that she spent as
if she *were Eugene and Nicole*. She would call me up and announce
we were going to a good restaurant where we wouldn't run into
anyone, somewhere like Peter Luger or Smith & Wollensky, and
that she was paying, usually in cash with tips from the restaurant, which she found hilarious, piling fives and tens on the white
tablecloth at Smith & Wollensky, and I would put on my best
approximation of a Weimar lesbian's outfit, and she would of
course dress like herself, which worked perfectly, and we would
have Bloody Marys, the only drink Rebecca actually liked. She
would drink three of them, three Bloody Marys, and then she
would have terrible heartburn, and say that this was why she
never drank alcohol, because alcohol always gave her heartburn,
and I would always tell her that it was the three glasses of tomato
juice mixed with horseradish that was giving her indigestion,
and that if she switched to something different like a martini she
would have a much nicer time, but then she would take her zip-
top LeSportsac bag of pills out and fish around in there and find
an Alka-Seltzer. She always had an Alka-Seltzer in her bag of
pills—this was how incredible my friend Rebecca was, she was
the most beautiful woman in the restaurant, and she always had
a loose Alka-Seltzer rattling around in an ancient LeSportsac
pencil case full of OxyContin bottles. I would offer to pay and

she would say *absolutely not, you child,* and I think, more than saying I was younger than her, she took great pleasure in enacting the childhood that she once had with her once beautiful, once wealthy mother, and so she would play mommy and pay for dinner and she would drink the Alka-Seltzer in one huge gulp and we would go home happy and full of steak. This was the kind of thing Alexander would say was a waste of your life. It's always the people who *don't know the value of a day's work* that are the quickest to stash their money away, I thought. It's always people like Alexander who are so afraid of working that they'll never spend a cent to enjoy themselves to keep from ever having to lift a finger. I found Alexander's behavior about money incredibly boring, though of course for the first few years of our friendship I was ruled by his opinions about money just as much as I was ruled by his taste, motivated by my preening desire for his approval. I looked across the table at Alexander, whose thick long black nose hairs were cascading out toward his lip like a nasal Pantene ad. It made me sick to recall the way that his approval of my writing was the most delicious prize for me in that period. If anything made me feel compassion for Nicole, I thought from my seat at the table, it was that she did not behave like Alexander when it came to money. Of course, money was like water to her. She needed to get more constantly and expel it, piss it away, at the same rate, but at least I was a beneficiary of her compulsive spending, and at least she had the decency to be ashamed of the way she spent money in the same way that I now realize Alexander was ashamed that he *did not have the money he thought he deserved.* Only recently, I thought, only recently, after my escape from Alexander, have I worked up the courage to resist caving in to the pathetic worldview he and other people like him have about money, about luxuries, this puritanical desire to refuse comfort, to view excess, or even something as regular as a three-day vacation, as a moral failing. You can spot a person like this from miles away by the grayness of their skin, the joylessness of their smile, and when I spotted someone like this I used to affect these features too. I would submit to their misery and I would pretend to be as joyless and judgmental and stoic and Victorian as they were. But now when I see these people I have a desire to provoke them, because I know that they're like Alexander, the children of doctors who wish they could have more, and I get this desire to make myself seem to them like des Esseintes in Huysmans's *À rebours*—they make me want to invent insane, perverse luxuries and speak only about bespoke curtains I'm having made from vicuña camel hair, or buying a lump of pure ambergris on the dark web, or having a living turtle's shell emblazoned with emeralds, because the only thing more *boring* than being materialistic is pretending you aren't. But I really had once loved Alexander so deeply. He was the first writer I had ever been friends with who actually *was a writer*. When I first met him he had only had a few stories published but they were in major magazines and they were good, if slightly overly adherent to the Lish disciple style of spare bleak minimalism that was a bit too in love with its own lower-middle-class references, as if rambling around a suburban Rite Aid looking for a tallboy of Coors

Banquet was so *bleak* and *depressing* that it could stand in for *anything happening in the story* because just by *rambling around a suburban Rite Aid looking for a tallboy of Coors Banquet* something like a great tragedy had been written. I also recall being impressed by the fact that he had an agent who he sometimes had to call on the phone or mail manuscripts to. Once we went over to the agent's apartment and babysat for her infant son, who had a Nordic name, something like Elvind or Ekdal, which delighted Alexander, as he told me, because she and her husband were both WASPs from the Midwest. But most importantly, which, as I sat in the loft on the Bowery looking at him, felt ridiculous and beyond belief, Alexander was the first person with whom I could have *interesting conversations about literature.* I shuddered now, sitting across from him at the table, remembering how I had looked at the bookshelf in his bedroom and said to him *wow, you're so incredibly well-read,* and the way that he had smiled kindly from his seat on the bed and said *experience comes with the advantage of having lived for a longer time,* and he patted the bed beside him, and afterward he gave me a few books to take home with me to read. I think they were Jean Rhys novels or Amy Hempel stories, they were definitely books by women. And he was also the first person who, after I'd admitted to him that I *wrote,* demanded to read my writing. He made me feel like I was a writer too, and I remember one night after leaving his apartment I went home and wrote a whole new story just for him to read. I had decided everything I had written so far was too juvenile for him to read, and so I wrote an entirely new piece just to show him, and I sent it to him and we talked about it the next day. He made me read it out loud to him, and we went over its strengths, and he gave me some suggestions, and then he told me that he would publish it in the next issue of a journal he edited with a wealthy patroness of the arts who I would meet that night at a dinner party, an artistic dinner party, in the very same room I was sat in now, where in that moment Eugene was in the process of spilling an entire glass of red wine onto the mushroom-colored carpet, possibly on purpose, and was laughing merrily with the young woman artist sitting next to him, holding her arms as he threw his little bald head back in laughter, as Nicole stared at him and then stood up, really making a performance out of it, pushing her chair back from the table with a screech and clomping across the room in her clogs, off to find some poor cater waiter on whom she could take out her frustration. I had often felt like what attracted Eugene to Nicole was her incredible willingness to be his patsy, that he could always get a rise out of her with his drunken antics, even when the rest of us had tired of paying him any attention when he became boorish and drunk. Eugene had boundless energy for making an ass of himself. I had noticed him making furtive trips to the bathroom, where he was no doubt revivifying himself with cocaine, as had always been his custom. Long after he should have been too drunk to function, he always kept himself motoring along with cocaine, long after his faculties of judgment, tact, and coordination had been dulled to the point of nonexistence he managed to soldier on as a tactless fool. Nicole returned to her place at the table and, still standing, raised her glass of wine. Dangling from her wrist was her delicate antique silver bracelet, a sort of mesh basket weave with little silver paillettes dangling from it. I hated recognizing it. I hated the intimacy between us that led me to knowing about what kind of jewelry Nicole wore. Everyone Nicole knew wore the same kind of jewelry. They were chunky-minimalist-silver-jewelry rich people, not layered-gold-necklaces rich people. This is an important distinction, again something I wish I didn't know about. Nicole had started speaking. She was thanking everybody for coming *today of all days*, she was saying that it was great to have everyone *liven up her home a bit*. She looked so small, Nicole, standing there over the table, presiding over the twenty or so *fabulous people* she'd managed to collect in her home. She wanted to look grand and magisterial, but instead she just looked kind of cute and little, the irony of course being that one of Nicole's prime life-goals was to shrink herself into sample size when the whole time she was actually broad-shouldered and regal. She was perpetually trying to whittle herself down into a physical shape that she was reaching now only as a consequence of her bones shriveling in late middle age. Nicole thanked the actress for coming and thanked the film producer, who was sat next to Nicole in a *seat of honor*, for introducing everyone. She said what fans she and Eugene were of the actress's work, what fans *we all were* of her work. I had never seen anything the actress was in, but of course I was happy to be registered as a nonentity at the table. Nicole continued. She said acting was one of the last great arts that people in this country still appreciated, and she was glad to have one of the best practitioners of that art sat at her table tonight, her table, which as everyone here knew, was meant to nourish and nurture the *greatest artistic minds in New York*. She then expressed *gratitude for the gifts from the earth that we are about to accept as nourishment*, which was a new one from Nicole, who was never religious, but then neither was this, it was some wacked-out eco-friendly woo-woo babble she clearly had picked up in the years since I had last seen her. Nicole had always flirted with the woo-woo, especially since there was no shortage of breathwork-teaching, floppy-hat-wearing, natural-dye-workshopping in Rhinebeck and the surrounding areas, but she did so with a wink, a healing tourmaline crystal used as a paperweight on a pile of bills, ketamine stored in a Tibetan singing bowl. Clearly something had happened while I was gone. I looked over at the actress, sitting at the other end of the table, next to Eugene. She had a face that was instantly familiar, not because I had seen her in anything or because she was so famous that her face was ubiquitous, but because she had this sort of featureless, regular face that is popular in films these days. I guess that's why people liked to cast her in films, because viewers would see her and instinctively be on her side because they'd subconsciously think, *her*, oh, I know her. They'd think, oh, she looks like my friend's older sister, or this girl I used to work with, or my uncommonly attractive second cousin, and so the filmmakers could skip the *making the protagonist likable* scenes and cut straight to the action. Rebecca was always going out on auditions for parts like this and it was no wonder why she never got them. Her face was so beautiful that it made people hate her, it made them fear her. She scared them. But she didn't want to go out and audition for the roles that better suited her—the sexy villains, the vamps. She wanted to be a *real actress*, a *leading lady*, which was perhaps another part of her elaborate plan to preclude herself from any chance at success. The actress was obviously a beautiful woman, I thought as I sat at the dining table, but she had none of Rebecca's magnetism. She had tiny little shoulders that wore her tiny little light pink Chanel tweed blazer. Rebecca would have really laughed at that, at the Chanel light pink tweed blazer, a *must-have*, as the subeditor at the fashion magazine would have called it, a *wardrobe staple* for people who know nothing about fashion but desperately want to show that they've *arrived*. But Rebecca of course would have killed for a light pink Chanel tweed blazer, not only because she'd have lusted after the object because of its price, but because these were the kinds of things young actresses got *paid to wear*, and so they were markers of success beyond their monetary value. Things that regular people had to pay high prices for, famous actresses got *paid* to wear, and she could never reconcile the fact that she was still in the category of paying customers. The blazer didn't look good on the actress. It looked too clean, too new. It looked like it may as well have still been wrapped in plastic and dangling from a dry-cleaning hanger. Rebecca would have done something to subvert the fustiness of the jacket, like putting cheap metal pins all over it, the kind that bands and political campaigns give out to their supporters, or she would have mussed up her hair, or

worn even more smeary black kajal eyeliner than usual, the way
that she would sometimes do when she'd get dressed and call her
outfit *dead* doll or *dead* nurse or *dead* Gibson Girl. The actress
just looked like she was a Republican from the 1980s who wanted
to look like she lived in Palm Beach but really lived in Houston.
The actress was carrying on across the table, throwing her head
back laughing in such a studied way, trying to show her *wild
abandon* in such a studious way, and I noticed that her hair wasn't
moving like normal hair would when someone threw their head
back. Her hair was staying put and it made her look like a space
alien or a robot version of a human woman until I noticed that
she actually had children's barrettes in her hair, no doubt an idea
from a stylist to help her *dress down* the blazer, but it was different
from the way Rebecca would have done it, it looked far too perfect, too planned. Rebecca would have assimilated the blazer
into her own wardrobe and made it look like she'd owned it forever. The actress's barrettes, which were color coordinated to
match the pink tweed, belied an insecurity, they were perfectly
placed accoutrements to further emphasize the jacket's novelty.
Women who wear things like children's barrettes in their hair
think that they are being *too quirky for words*, that they're *so cute*
no one can *take it*. They're wearing something *made for children*
but they're *grown-ups*! Ha-ha. How wild, how *transgressive*, how
positively boring. I watched as Alexander tried to finagle his way
into the conversation Eugene was having in hushed tones with
the actress, but they did not hear him, which was surprising because everyone else could easily make out the nasal, booming

*well actually*s and *that really reminds me of*s that came from his
seat at the table. These went unnoticed only by the actress and
by Eugene, and so as everyone else looked at him, Alexander
concealed his humiliation by bringing his soup spoon to his
mouth and pretending he hadn't said anything at all. Alexander
was so used to being the central artist at these Eugene-and-
Nicole dinners, especially ever since his second novel was published to *great critical acclaim*, and it was delightful watching him
suffer the worst possible indignity that he could imagine: being
overlooked by the actress, someone who he believed should have
recognized him as her equal in celebrity and her superior in intellect. I remembered when I had wanted to become Alexander's
*equal* so badly, when I thought of his circumstances as my goals,
and the elation I felt when finally Alexander had published my
piece in his journal—I had opened to the table of contents and
was delighted to see my name printed among fiction writers
whose books I had read in the library at Eugene and Nicole's, the
work of people that I admired. I had flipped to the page that contained my story and I had found something that *resembled* my
story. Something that was *similar* to my story in content. But I
had found that the *editor*, Alexander, had rewritten every sentence to more closely resemble his style. He had excised from the
story anything that sounded like something I would write and
had published instead a story that mined the content of my life
but was formally in every way his. Nicole came back from the
kitchen, carrying a mason jar full of murky brown liquid as one
of the caterers set a large earthenware bowl full of greens on the

table. She sat down and lifted the mason jar high and announced *this is Alexander's recipe for salad dressing*, which was her way of announcing that she had slept with Alexander many times. When someone thanks someone else *for their salad dressing recipe* it is invariably meant to announce that they have had sex with the person. And the way that Alexander somewhat sheepishly smiled at no one in particular, at all of the guests, in recognition of the fact that he was the genitor of the recipe for the salad dressing, as Nicole vigorously shook the jar to re-emulsify its contents, confirmed everything that she had more or less said. Nicole always needed everyone to know that she had sex with people besides Eugene. Or rather, Nicole always needed everyone to know that other people found her sexually attractive. I'm not sure if she found the need to hint *subtly* at the fact that she slept with other people because of her desire to put a semiotic distance between her *self* and that of her boorish, humiliating *man*, or if it was Nicole's way of asserting that she was *desirable*, her way of announcing to a tableful of people that *multiple people currently seated at that table desired her* or, of course, at one point had been beaten down enough, at one point had been drunk enough, to have succumbed to her advances. I watched as she shook the jar of dressing, her wrist really gyrating more than it needed to, she was really swiveling that mason jar around her arm with a sort of limp, sort of slack gesture, she was really emulsifying that mustard-miso mixture that *Alexander had taught her about*, really going *crazy emulsifying it*, really making such a spectacle of mixing together the dressing. It was clear that she was desperate to hold the attention of the room, and she was so terribly dull that the only way she could think to do this was by shaking a fucking maraca of oil and vinegar around. Nicole found herself totally irresistible, and this was what made her so repellent. She was quite beautiful, despite her best efforts at making herself totally gruesome through her behavior. She had always been quite beautiful. When I first fell under her influence I found her to be exceptionally elegant. I also found the way she was undisturbed by Eugene's active pursuit of other women to be so evolved, the way she seemed to not even think about middle-class constructs of fidelity and propriety, and meanwhile she was so *elegant*, she was so self-assured, she could sit in the same room as Eugene and his prey and remain genuinely *cool*. And though this may seem unremarkable, I found it awe-inspiring that she was the only person I'd ever seen wear a French-twist hairstyle and look *cool*, I remembered as I sat at the dinner table. She was the only person who could wear that signature of librarians and schoolteachers, the *French-twist* hairstyle, and look not only *elegant* but *interesting*. How on earth, I had thought, could this woman who is able to make a French twist, secured with a silver hairpin, look so *modern*, how on earth could someone with her grace, her originality, be disrespected by someone like Eugene? But at that time, I thought, I was thinking only in the terms of my own bourgeois morality, and it seemed as though she had enough romance of her own to keep her entertained—romances that were less frequent, less public, and longer lasting and there-fore, somehow, truer, and I admired the way she comported herself so I would come to her for advice about my own affairs. Or rather, I was always with her and so she would offer her advice unprompted, as she had taken it upon herself to *guide me*, and she would offer the advice through *possibly witty* aperçu that I didn't fully understand, like, *you don't only have one hairbrush, do you?* And I would cherish this advice, though I had no idea what it meant with regards to my romantic life. I also actually did only have one hairbrush, and I became unsure if I should purchase another hairbrush, and what the purpose of this expanded wardrobe of hairbrushes *would be*. Usually these audiences with Nicole were private, Eugene taking no part in the advice giving. I had been sure to keep him out of any personal confidences after learning, quickly after meeting him, that he told everybody everything. This was fun when you got to hear about the intimate lives of his famous friends and more fun when he recounted pathetic stories about people I had just met and thought highly of, like a woman who had been at one of the dinner parties and was talking about Czech cinema with great authority and interest. This woman had managed to discuss the films without the pedantry *film people* usually force on you, and she actually said that a number of art-house masterpieces were *totally worthless* if you're actually interested in *enjoying* yourself. I found that frankness, that bravery charming, so I complimented her to Eugene after she left, saying you could tell that she was the rare person involved in film who actually seemed to take pleasure in simply *watching movies* and not in ticking off films from a list. He responded by saying this was true, and then, slowly tracing his finger around the rim of his cocktail glass and crossing his legs as he sat on my friend, the white sofa, looked down as if he were debating divulging something *spicy*, which of course he wasn't, he was always going to say whatever he wanted to, until he looked up and finally said she was an absolute nutcase who had flown from Los Angeles to Marfa to see a man she had met online, a married screen-printing artist in his late sixties, who it turned out had a sexual fetish for pooping on women, and that his friend, the cinephile, had allowed the screen-printing artist to poop on her, and had ended up loving it so much that she became obsessed with the screen-printing artist, and after a week together she moved from Los Angeles to Marfa to be with him without asking, assuming that he would want this, and when it transpired that he did not want to leave his wife and poop on her in a more permanent arrangement, she began stalking him. She was so in love with him that she could not spend more than a few hours away from him, and began showing up at his adobe *casita*, banging on the windows and, eventually, lighting a bag of feces on fire outside his door! Like in the movies! Eugene and I agreed, after he told me that story, that we respected the cinephile even more for hearing this story, and he said, *oh, that's just the beginning with her. That's why I keep her around. For the stories.* Ever since he said that, that he *keeps her around for the stories*, I've been careful not to tell Eugene the smallest bit about my life. But Nicole I confided everything in, Nicole I trusted with almost anything. I remember once, when I had taken the train up to Rhinebeck to meet Nicole and Eugene, around six months after

Rebecca had taken up with her Chess Player and disappeared from our lives, Eugene had said that I looked sad and I denied it and Nicole said, leaning against a floor-to-ceiling window, in her languid, smoke-deepened voice, *who said that time heals all wounds? It would be better to say that time heals everything except wounds. With time, the desired body will soon disappear, and if the desiring body has already ceased to exist for the other, then all that remains is a wound, disembodied.* What a beautiful concept, I remembered thinking. No wonder Nicole and Eugene had such an open and honest relationship, even with all the infidelity, when Nicole had such an incredible power for understanding pain and longing and jealousy and betrayal. I remembered this line, a line I thought was the most beautiful thing that I had ever heard. I wasn't sure that I understood it, or if it applied to my relationship with Rebecca at all, or, like all her advice, if it was advice of any kind, but I thought that this was real poetry from Nicole. I wrote this line down in my diary the moment I went up to my room to deposit the military-surplus duffel bag I still use to this day, that I purchased with Rebecca at that place on Delancey Street, that bag that I've taken everywhere with me since I bought it, a piece of Rebecca with me everywhere that I've been. I took my diary out of that bag and wrote Nicole's quotation down in one of the orange spiral flip-top notebooks with gridded pages that I've always been partial to, copying it out as closely as I could remember it, and I would revisit this quote occasionally when I would feel somewhat heartbroken, and I would feel so lucky that I was friends with someone as brilliant as Nicole, who could say things so clever and poignant and sad. Years later I went to see the film *Sans Soleil* at the Metrograph, one of those downtown establishments that caters so well to your desires as a young sybarite that it makes you feel ashamed of yourself, how they stock kombucha in the refreshment stand next to tastefully designed boxes of candy, and you think *this is exactly what I want*, which makes you want to kill yourself, truly. I went to the Metrograph for a retrospective they did for Chris Marker's one hundredth birthday, and I fell in love with the film *Sans Soleil*, or *Sunless*—and with the deep husky voice of the narrator, sort of like Nicole's voice. It was really one of the best films I'd ever seen, a montage of disconnected images that was such a beautiful meditation on time, on memory, on culture. It was the total inverse of when Eugene put on *Koyaanisqatsi* in Rhinebeck while we were all on ketamine, which was one of the most disorienting, even scariest experiences of my life, to feel confused and dissociated as images of destruction and oppression flashed across the flat-screen TV and the undulating Philip Glass score boomed in surround sound from *the Sonos system*, all the while with Eugene and Nicole sitting on either side of the sofa, feeding me key bumps of ketamine. I shuddered in the theater remembering the feeling that *Koyaanisqatsi* produced: that the world was *out of order*, just as its title said, in the Hopi language that was all but *wiped out* by manifest destiny, by industrialization, by the rich, by the ancestors of Eugene's collectors, one would imagine, but also that the film, through its judgmental Western gaze, elevated the *real life* of the *primitive cultures* in a way that was humiliating, and I made a mental note as I sat in the theater to revisit the film in a sober state, when I could discern the floor from the ceiling. Meanwhile, as I was watching *Sans Soleil*, I felt as though Marker had shown, through a similarly Orientalizing but less didactic gaze, that there was an unspeakable tenderness that pervaded life on earth, that even in moments of great tragedy, human beings made carnivals, visited shrines, held hands on buses, and I thought that I needed to show this film to Nicole and Eugene. Or rather, by this point in my friendship with them I had learned merely to mention that I had seen it, because to recommend something to them that they already knew about was inviting upon yourself one of Nicole's signature looks, a look like a pat on the head to a well-meaning, ignorant child, a child who has picked all of the best perennials out from the garden for a bouquet for Mommy. And then, around halfway through the movie, I heard the exact line that Nicole had said to me years before in Rhinebeck, the line about *time healing everything except wounds*, and I thought *maybe I am going crazy*, maybe I'd misremembered what Nicole had said, but I knew I hadn't because I'm blessed with a perfect memory that only seems to have gotten *better* as I've gotten older, just as my facility with foreign languages has also only *improved* as I've gotten older. I'm particularly good at remembering both the uncharacteristically brilliant and the strikingly moronic things that people say, and so I could barely concentrate for the last third of the film because I was so busy wondering if Nicole had given me advice that was really just lifted from Chris Marker's video essay, and then I began wondering what the implications of that were—if that made me respect her more for memorizing a passage of beautiful language from a wonderful film, or if it made me feel afraid of her, disgusted by her, and then I worried that perhaps my memory had begun to fail me, that she hadn't said that at all, that she had said something that contained those ideas, that resembled it, but that was something else entirely, and I thought about it ceaselessly in the theater, so much so that I couldn't concentrate at all on the last third of the film. I walked back home like a madwoman in a Groucho Marx trot, and I found the orange spiral notebook that corresponded to the time I'd visited her in Rhinebeck, and I flipped through the pages to where I had written the exact passage that I'd heard on film, attributed to Nicole in my tight little handwriting. This upset me deeply. Quoting from a poem without attribution is normal, if a bit twee, so I wondered why I cared so much about Nicole regurgitating the quote, why it bothered me so much that she hadn't told me that the quote was from something else. And I realized, as I sat hunched over my notebook in my small Brooklyn apartment, that it was because when she had said those words to me in the house in Rhinebeck I felt as though she had really thought deeply about the advice she planned to give me. I felt as though she had deeply understood and cared for me. But instead I felt like she was more interested in demonstrating her knowledge of culture, in dipping into her own cultural memory—that rather than offering me any real comfort she was, as always, *locked in cultural exchange with herself.* It was a reminder that I had everything I'd thought I wanted, I was friends with artists, and

lived in their *alternative bohemian* world, my friends could quote
from something like a Chris Marker film and knew about interesting books and laughed at people who waited in lines for highly
rated pizza places and still, these friends, Nicole and her louse of
a *man*, had never done anything but use me, especially that night
in Rhinebeck when she quoted the Marker, that night when I
was so drunk and disoriented and sad—that had really been the
night—and then, from my perch at the table, I looked at Nicole's
bloated body and I couldn't bear to think about that night years
ago in Rhinebeck when I finally capitulated to them, or *gave into
my desires*, as I'm sure Nicole thought of it. Nicole really did need
to think that everybody was attracted to her, and I was grateful
that the Mediterranean spread was being served to interrupt my
memory, the platters of dips and spreads and little scrumptious
delicacies tarted up and dusted with herbs and dotted with edible
flowers. I watched as the actress, who was sat next to Eugene in
the center of the table, helped herself to a portion of the fish roe.
Everyone was silent as she scraped the side of the platter for the
fish roe, and from the way that people looked at her with a sort
of anticipatory gaze, I realized that while I'd been suffering from
my memories, she had been holding forth to the rest of the table
for quite some time. She was talking about a film that she had
starred in. Her role, she said, was incredibly difficult to prepare
for because she'd had to gain a bit of weight to play a government employee who was depressed and crazed and, though she
had an incredibly powerful position in the government, was psy-
chopathically jealous of her more beautiful older sister. *I can't*

*imagine*, Nicole said. *Hollywood is such a crazy place if someone who looks like you has to play the ugly sister. I would be so offended if they called me up to say you've got the job! You were perfect. You ARE the ugly sister.* The actress smiled. *That's very kind of you but I actually only auditioned for that role. I wanted to play Claire, the so-called ugly sister,* she said, *because it was such a wonderful part. I really had to argue for it, because the director couldn't see me as someone who not only is so physically repulsive but also has an external appearance that had made her live a life of jealousy, rejection, and bitterness, leading her to do the sickening things she does in the film. But that was exactly why I wanted to do the role,* the actress said, *because I don't think our behavior is tied to the way that we look. I wanted to prove that with the film.* Alexander looked up from his empty plate. *Well, then why did you play an ugly person who is evil instead of one who looks more like yourself? Doesn't that just prove that you think people who are bad-looking are bad? Shouldn't you have played the villain as the thin, beautiful woman that you are?* Alexander smiled at the actress. His favorite way of flirting was calling women beautiful idiots, as I knew well. I also knew it often worked. I sipped on a *pea flower Collins* that one of Nicole's *little helpers* had distributed to pair with the spread. It tasted kind of bad, but in a good way, like purple Gatorade that had been spiked with wheatgrass and gin. *No,* the actress said. *We have all kinds of representations of beautiful women as villains. The femme fatale is one of the oldest archetypes in cinema. So I didn't mind that the writer had conceived of the character that way. It did offend me that, because I could play ingenues, they thought that I wouldn't be able to capture this kind of twisted, revolting person. But I knew that I could make myself into a really foul person. What was the point of all my training if all I ever needed to do was look pretty? It was more of an artistic challenge than a political statement.* She smiled in a way that lit up her undeniably pretty face, as if to say, *if I had a sister, no one would think I'm the ugly one.* Nicole nodded solemnly from the other side of the table to prove that she was listening. The pea flower Collins was vintage Nicole. I was still drinking it, because it tasted like nothing I'd ever had before, which isn't to say it was good. The reason certain flavors are commonly available is because they taste good. The drink reminded me of the time Nicole had commissioned an artist to bake a honey cake for Eugene's birthday and the artist had decorated it with purple flowers and frosted it with white buttercream that looked like it had speckles of high-quality vanilla bean in it, or maybe cocoa shavings, but actually the buttercream was flavored with a handful of dirt from the garden where the bees had foraged for pollen to make their honey. After I tasted it I remembered Nicole gave me a pleading look, as if she hoped I would then convey that I didn't think the cake was a disaster, that I thought the cake was postmodern and interesting seeming, just like the *birthday boy* Eugene. I remembered the pathetic way she looked at me, encouraging me to pretend that the texture actually added something nice to the experience, and it absolutely did add to the experience, in a way. I mean, Nicole had given us an incredibly rare experience, having a delicious and light honey cake in your mouth that you were attempting to enjoy while simultaneously trying to ignore the gritty texture of dirt, toward which I'm sure the human body has evolved the instinct of disgust to recognize something we should not consume. Nicole swore that she hadn't known the artist was going to put dirt all over the cake, but I wasn't sure if that was true. She had chosen the artist to make the cake precisely because she discovered this artist through a *relational aesthetics* piece they did at PS1 in which they served pigs' hearts marinated in yuzu vinegar and fermented sheep scrotum in hollow coconut shells to some of the world's biggest collectors, and so I hoped that she had worked with this artist because she knew they would make something like a dirt cake, because if she had, it was one of Nicole's greatest strokes of genius, a rare moment of self-awareness. Everything, I thought as I sat at the dinner table, at Nicole and Eugene's was like a perfectly made cake flavored with dirt. I let the pea flower Collins make me drunk. *I had spent so long wanting the role*, the actress said, *that I hadn't realized how much work I would need to do once I got it. In order to prepare for the role I had to put myself under so much physical stress. It was absolutely exhausting. I had to gain the weight, and no one will admit it but it's so difficult as a working actress*, she said, *because as a working actress you never know what role you're going to get next, when the most important part of your career is going to come up, and at the time this film was what I wanted, but what if there was something else that needed me to be in perfect shape coming after it? So as I was following the weight gain plan, with each peanut butter milkshake I had I felt closer to Claire, to the character that I was inhabiting, who used food as a source of comfort, but I also knew that was an extra eight hundred calories I'd have to run off later, when I wanted to get back to normal, that the body I have always been lucky enough to have was something I'd soon have to work for. Actually, this tension was what let me unlock the secret of the character, what let me understand the shame and desperation of people who look like that, whose bodies are out of their control, and I think,* the actress said, pausing to have a long sip of wine, *that's what allowed me to give such an embodied performance.* Alexander was opening his mouth to say something every time the actress paused for air, but she continued before he managed to let out a noise. He was tapping his fork on the table lightly, rapping it against the tablecloth rapidly and quietly to bring attention to himself without that seeming like his intention. I could tell Alexander was desperate to bring this monologue by the actress to an end, not only because he probably found what she was saying to be asinine, but also because it offended him that she was allowed to bloviate about her work whereas, in my experience, he was usually stopped from having self-contained debates with himself about his own books at the dinner table. *Even though it took me six months before I could get back to fighting weight,* she said, *it was completely worth it because I had the chance to embody the ideas of one of the few truly brilliant directors left in America.* Alexander dropped the fork. *Brilliant?* he said. *Brilliant? You think that director is brilliant?* I wasn't sure what director they meant, but clearly Alexander and everyone else knew because the other guests went quiet and the film producer looked up from Clara Carson's tits for the first time all night. It seemed like although most people were used to Alexander's need to be the *moral compass* of all interactions, the steward of the group's *soul*, it felt like he had been waiting to joust with her from the start and she appeared a bit too *fragile* for him to take aim at her before the main course. But I could tell that this was not at all who she was. She was quite strong, ruthless. *Oh please*, the actress said, unfazed by Alexander's whiny voice, *don't tell me you actually give credence to any of the ridiculous fake-feminist circus around him.* Alexander rolled his eyes. *His well-documented rapes aren't what I'd call a fake-feminist circus.* At first I thought she was talking about our mutual acquaintance, the director with the permanently soiled baseball cap, but then I realized how I'd recognized the actress: from an article I'd skimmed about the newest film of a widely canceled geriatric American auteur. They said that the director had abandoned all that had made him interesting to cineastes and had wound up making the type of stylistically bland and pandering Hollywood film that his earlier work had critiqued. I wondered why this actress had decided to accept a part in the film when that director was obviously a toxic entity to associate with, though I guessed it was because she wanted to differentiate herself from the twenty or so other actresses of her cohort who had emerged with her, neck and neck as *potential A-list stars*, and pull ahead by doing something none of them would deign to do, all while making herself known to the more *intellectual* film world. Alexander continued, *but that's not my problem with him, I don't think an artist's work should be criticized based on its maker's actions, but I do think that it has become so easy to hide behind being canceled for violent conduct to avoid a rebuke of your art. It isn't because he's allegedly raped people that I think his films are bad. In saying let the art speak for itself, you're actually hiding from the critique of the art. I think his art is bad. I think it's shocking that young independent producers decided he was the sagacious voice of the past that needed to be re-amplified, that it was a mistake to have left him in the previous century languishing for his crimes, that they needed to throw their credibility and money behind him to let him continue making his half-baked art with the message of nihilism and the aesthetic power of nada that lets unintelligent people congratulate themselves for going to the smaller independent movie theater where they play art-house and foreign films so that they can think they're witnesses to high art. His films are nostalgic for a high-testosterone exploitative America in a way that I find fascist, totally fascist. They purport to critique that culture but all they do is reify a very obvious longing that the director and his fans have to be rich, culture-less capitalists. If I wanted to see rich people on TV I'd turn on the news.* Alexander leaned back into his seat comfortably and swirled the liquid in his glass. The actress nodded slowly, looking down at her plate. *Oh no,* she said, *his films teach people things about what is going on in the world. It could be that I know less about the world than you, but I learned what a leveraged buyout is, how corporate governance works, what the World Bank's role is from one of his films. And that was just from watching it. I've never learned more on a set than I did on his film. I had to shadow an undersecretary at the Fed.* Nicole softly rapped her chunky silver ring on the table twice in agreement, which she did often, the globular ring was sort of like her shiny, wearable gavel. *I learned soooo much from that movie!* Nicole said, and Alexander laughed at her, either because the way she said *that movie* was proof she had no idea what the actress was talking about or because the idea of Nicole learning tickled him. Nicole pushed her chair slightly away from the table, as if to stand up and leave, though no one thought she would really get up and leave, and I felt sorry in that moment for Nicole, remembering suddenly that this remained her life, that dinners with Eugene and Alexander had remained the *mainstays of her everyday life*, that these dinners were not *evenings she had to endure* but rather what *made up her life*. At one point I too had *oriented my life* around these dinners, and it embarrassed me to think about the way I would wait eagerly to hear what Alexander had to say. Alexander, who always wanted to believe he was *engaged in political discourse*. According to Alexander he didn't like *gossip*, or small talk, he didn't enjoy *idle chitchat*. In his mind the reason that he attended dinner parties was to *engage in political discourse*. The main problem with this was the fact that Alexander knew practically nothing about politics, history, or what went on in the world *aside from* gossip. Alexander's primary interest was and had always been American literature, women, and gossip, particularly about women: who had them, who didn't deserve them, and which ones he wanted. In his mind, perhaps, he managed to transform those conversations about women into *political ones*, by talking about the *radical theories* some *brilliant woman* had exposed him to or the *reactionary chauvinism* of the *brilliant woman's* boyfriend. He did, however, have a nearly encyclopedic knowledge of twentieth-century American literature, but aside from those books, Alexander *proudly* told people that he knew nothing about the world. He had gone to a decent university in New York where he had studied *only American literature*, and at one point he had been tremendously proud of this fact. When we were first friends and he had not yet published his novel, he had told me this about his education as though knowledge of anything aside from American literature would preclude him from being an expert and eventual practitioner in it. To his credit, when Alexander talked about literature, you could tell that he truly loved books, that he invested great importance in novels, and that figuring out why certain novels *worked* and what was at the *core of them* was important to him. And yet when we were so close, when I walked over to his apartment in Brooklyn every day for what I think we both viewed as my lessons, I found discussing books with him to be painful and confusing. I loved the books that he suggested to me and allowed me to borrow, but the moment we began to discuss them, I found myself befuddled. It was often as if we had read completely different books. At first, because he spoke with such authority, his deep whiny voice always ending on a *downbeat*, suggesting that anyone who didn't agree with him had not actually understood something so manifestly obvious that they must be a moron, and because I trusted his authority on literature, because I was so young and felt ignorant for having forgone a classic literary education, and because I had been inside his apartment and seen the floor-to-ceiling shelves that contained so many books I felt like I was *supposed to* have read already, I always felt as though he had understood something deeper within the novel that I had been unable to find. For someone so in love with literature, however, he was incredibly resistant to reading anything outside of this American syllabus he had created for himself to master and then, eventually, enter. I would occasionally recommend books that I had loved to him—Victorian novels, Russian literature, and some French novels that were my favorites—but he had told me that he wasn't interested in things that old because they would have no bearing on his style. He also would never read anything in translation because he said he had so much *prose in the original* to get through. I remember feeling hurt by this when he said it, hurt and like an idiot for having wasted so much time on prose written by translators, but I knew that those books were important to me. A few weeks before I cut myself off from him we had gone to a dinner party full of writers, and a tall PhD student with hair like Beethoven had been talking about how much he enjoyed reading Proust and suggested that Alexander would love the social drama of Madame Verdurin—that in fact Alexander's friends Eugene and Nicole were a bit like the Verdurins—and Alexander had told Beethoven his beliefs about the idiocy of reading literature in translation. This was the first time that I didn't want people to associate me with Alexander, when Dr. Beethoven had said that Alexander, by closing himself off from Proust and Dostoyevsky because he couldn't read French and Russian, was only reading imitations of their styles by authors in his native tongue. I remember he said that the same people

Alexander was reading in the *so-called original* were ripping off the styles, ideas, and literary techniques of the continental writers, so by rejecting the translations and reading American authors so that he could experience the author's original thoughts, what he was really doing was experiencing an even smaller fraction of the original literary idea of some movement than he would by reading the author in translation—that actually Alexander's method was sort of like reading only Murakami to understand *The Catcher in the Rye*. I don't remember what Alexander said to the PhD student, but I remember this was the moment when I knew I had to get away from his influence. I had suspected so many of Alexander's ironclad pronouncements to be idiotic, and to have this windswept stranger confirm my suspicions gave me the confidence to throw off Alexander, who I had once worshipped as the greatest fount of wisdom, who had completely dominated me. Alexander, who I had at one point been so in love with that I gleefully read drafts of his novel in which every other character had a name but the character based on me was referred to only as *the nineteen-year-old* even though actually I was twenty-three at that point. Who I had admired so much that I showed him every single thing I wrote, the only one who I allowed to see what I had written. Alexander, who, when I began to have the smallest amount of literary success, inveighed against the journals that had published me with such ardor and enthusiasm that I believed him and thought that my publications were useless. Alexander, whose judgment was my only authority, and who meted out his approval so rarely that it often served only to crush me when it did come, because he approved only of things that I felt were minor accomplishments, in a way that made me feel like he thought so little of me that he was amazed by my doing the most pathetic things. Only when I heard Dr. Beethoven make such a lucid case against him, a case that resembled my own submerged opinion of Alexander's beliefs, was I able to allow myself to think in earnest the thoughts about him that had been simmering in the back of my mind. Only then, when I saw him for how ridiculous he was, was I able to untether myself from his influence, never to return to his Brooklyn apartment. I had not seen Alexander again until now, at this table at Eugene and Nicole's, in this basement of the human spirit that he had first dragged me along to years ago. I had ignored him completely after that night, and I had been shocked when he hardly put up any resistance to my exit from his life, because in truth I had left not only to protect myself from his deranged thoughts but also as a sort of show of my independence: to show that I was able to exist as a person, a thinker, without him. That I was not *the nineteen-year-old* of his writing but a real person who could navigate the world on my own, who could navigate the world better than he could. At first I had wanted him to beg for my return, to ask me to accompany him to museums and readings and parties, and I had imagined the great pleasure I would take in refusing him, but after the first few signs of detachment, when I didn't reply to a link to a news article or to a meme that he had sent me, he stopped messaging me altogether. I had wanted a conflict in which I could tell him how stupid he was, how self-involved, rude, and stupid he was—a confrontation in which I could take back every simpering comment I had made about his intellect—and then I received an apologetic email from an editor of a well-respected journal rescinding the acceptance of my story because they had overfilled the issue. A subsequent private text message from an intern at the magazine, who I had met at a gallery opening, later explained that the now-famous Alexander had threatened to pull his story if mine was included. I should have been upset when I saw that he was behind this serious setback but instead it made me laugh. I was laughing and celebrating, I remembered, as I sat across from Alexander at the table in Eugene and Nicole's house, I was laughing because he was so threatened by the idea that I was *on his level*, that I was his *equal*, that he'd exercised his power to see me removed from the publication. Of course, it did eventually annoy me that Alexander was sabotaging my literary career from his position as the new darling of an asinine media-centric literary culture that valued authors who wrote only of the literary media and its gossip so that the literary media would have no choice but to review their novels, delivering readers to them regardless of their quality, their ideas, and their style, to say nothing of their entertainment value. But still, it heartened me to know that my departure from Alexander's life had wounded him so thoroughly that he felt the need to sabotage me, and it took a long while for me to kill the urge to wound him back. I had never considered using the auspices of certain so-called feminist sex-panic movements to try to destroy his career, although I had many stories of things he'd done to me that were far worse than what I'd seen on a document being sent around by women I knew. Of course, some of the so-called movement did address the sexual violence that is an undercurrent in our society, but many of the subsequent *lists* were full of *acts*, that, though they were undoubtably uncomfortable and unpleasant, I felt amounted to little more than *regrets*, regrets for interactions that women had played an active part in and now wished they could suddenly take back. They wanted to hide behind being the *weaker sex* to punish these men who had wronged them using score-settling in the professional sphere, and reprimand them through barring them from work success, as if that was a balm for violence. It was offensive to women who had actually experienced genuine violence *and* to women who believed they were adults who could sit and live with the consequences of their own actions. I didn't need to be *protected* from the things that had happened to me, and if I did, I wouldn't want that protection to be someone getting fired from their job, I'd want something much worse to happen to them. No, I found it much more satisfying to hold the anvil over Alexander's head than to drop it, to be able to catch his glance while he performed his role as a *socially conscious man* who was *interested in women's empowerment* and cause him to writhe under the weight of his own memories. Alexander was still lecturing the actress about the emptiness of her recent film, about its artlessness and its obsession with money and the rich. He was telling her about his theory that art should have a political valence that trended toward the left or else it was better left unmade—that it was better not to find an audience than to find an audience made up of people enslaved to capital and to glamour, as her work had done. The actress nodded politely and said *Are you finished?* Alexander laughed. *Yes, I'm finished. I apologize, actually. I don't know what got into me there. There's really no point in talking about any of this with you, I got so carried away. There's no point in getting bogged down in all of this with you, it's not as if you wrote the film. I think we should just enjoy Nicole's spread and speak only of nice things. We probably don't have very much to say to each other, when it comes to all this. Let's just enjoy our cocktails and our vegetables and what's left of our youth.* The actress smiled at Alexander and said slowly *Yes, maybe we should stop talking about anything substantive. I was nervous to come here with Eric*—she gestured at the film producer—*because I thought, you know, people say New York intellectuals and art world people are so smart and they're going to think I'm just this stupid actress from LA. But that's exactly why I wanted to come here. Because I'm honestly very interested in art and literature and politics and I often wish that in LA I had more people to talk about those things with, not to say that no one in LA is smart, but I do find myself sometimes just talking about my career with my friends, even the ones who are brilliant and also read and write and are interested in things. I think there's something about the whole city being a part of the industry that makes people by default start to talk about their latest project and see who you know, so that they can tell you who they know, people who are also just talking about their careers, and their projects, and we're all just exchanging the names of bodyworkers and hair people, talking about box office performance and gossiping about who got certain parts and how our careers are going, and it really is true no one reads the newspaper there, and so I was actually kind of excited to come to New York with Eric because I always think of New York as a place that's different—actually my friend once got me this coffee mug that says* too stupid for New York too ugly for LA, *which I've always cherished, but I was excited to be too stupid for New York! I was excited to be around people who I could really talk to about art and books, which in LA usually devolves into a discussion about optioning the book, talking about if the book should be a film or if it's more of a TV show, and I've spent some time in New York but honestly just with other movie people, and that's why I wanted to do my next movie with Eric in the first place because I knew that he was tapped into a whole world of interesting people that had no idea who I was and didn't care about the very specific drama that revolves around other early career actresses like myself and just could talk to me about books. I wanted to immerse myself in a more intellectual scene than the one I was used to, where people pay consultants to buy books for their libraries and then organize them by the color of their spines. But meeting you*—and here she didn't look at Alexander but rather down at her plate—*confirms that I should have listened to my television writer friends who told me I was wrong about New York. They always talk about how they avoided the left-wing horseshoe-theory pseudo-artistic scene, or whatever you want to call it. I was suspicious of the way they said that in the rarefied artistic world of New York, if you're actually making anything for real people, rather just critiquing, criticizing, having your little takes, people think you're an idiot.*

*At first I didn't believe them, because they write for spy thriller streamer shows, so I thought maybe the people they met were right to think they weren't all that intellectual. But I get this sense that it's bigger than having a problem with the material itself. I really have been noticing, especially among the younger crowd I've met in New York during my visit, that if you are genuinely interested in a project there are these nihilistic people who want to make you feel like they have some kind of rich alternative inner life, some kind of nobler life because they aren't interested in traditional success, when actually, neither are you, you're interested in trying to make art, but they manage to turn this into some careerist judgment about you, that their nihilism, which is actually just a lack of success, means that they are purer, that they have access to a secret world of rich inner meaning that you do not. What they are really interested in is the feeling of superiority you get when you play your cards so close to your chest you forget that you're even playing.* The actress took another helping of the arugula that lined the platter of chicken Milanese. Alexander attempted to interrupt her at various moments, no doubt to explain that he was actually quite interested in *making work*, that she may not *read much* so she may not know that he is a *novelist* and that *novel writing* takes lots of work. That he'd won many *awards* for his writing, and made lots of *money* as well. He would likely have said that he shared her feelings about the critical yet lazy downtown set, that his work ethic was one of his proudest attributes, but the actress didn't leave him space to interrupt. *I understand it actually. Before I was successful I was critical like that,* she said. *I was incredibly critical of everyone I knew who was making low-budget films and submitting them to festivals. It made me sick the way they instrumentalized their most precious, most intimate memories, their relationship to their grandmother, their ethnic holidays, their childhood traumas to make these sentimental, bland, and pathetic films.* She sipped her wine. *I was critical of the actors who had small parts in films—parts I now can admit I would have killed for at the time—and posted their three-second appearances to their social media. I thought they looked like idiots two times, first by acting in something awful, and then by seeming proud of a tiny appearance on a dinky web series and promoting it as if it mattered. I was studying literature at the time and I was even critical of the people publishing novels about their lives, about every detail of their boring, middle-class lives, whether they were self-flagellating accounts of their guilt about living in a consumer society or unfiltered accounts of a life on the margins. Those always made me laugh the hardest, the idea that people who spent their time living in New York doing drugs and partying were busy writing autofiction about it, and that we were meant to believe that this made them interesting. Maybe*—she ate a forkful of arugula—*maybe I was fair to have a complete distaste for those writers, and for the most part I find that kind of writing quite pathetic, I mean the stuff that calls itself autofiction, the authors that self-identify as writers of autofiction,* she said, and I watched Alexander, the great autofiction writer at the table, saw slowly through his chicken Milanese. The actress waved her fork around. *I really don't mind the actual stuff that's in their books, like, okay whatever, have fun going to the farmers market and then having a disappointing date with someone from an app,* she said, *what* *bothers me is their urge to make anything they do content for their book, which is actually the same kind of obsession with success, but that by doing it as a book with some kind of autofiction artistic form or whatever they are somehow different or better than me and my friends who they see as careerist bimbos for making entertaining and interesting content that people might actually enjoy. But then, honestly, when my own career started to take off I stopped being so critical. I reconsidered, and thought about how the authors might really be interested in producing like . . . a record of existence . . . in the now— which even if it's self-indulgent and bland is all we can really try to accomplish on this earth—and I then realized that I actually knew a lot of people who hated those writers, hated those filmmakers, hated basically anyone who made anything. They were other young sceney kids who went to screenings in LA, went to the one fake club night at this restaurant that everyone in the LA scene converged on, and the only thing they were able to present as an alternative was a kind of nihilistic belief that doing nothing or doing drugs all day was better. And they really sold you on this idea because of their innate charisma and their strange outfits I didn't understand. They were so charismatic that they actually managed to convince me that there was something important about what they were doing, which was nothing. But when I thought about it they didn't really believe that opting out of making something was more interesting, no, they were just jealous that other people had been able to do what they themselves wanted to do so badly that they couldn't even try. And it hurt them that those people who'd succeeded actually weren't stuck-up losers, people who had, like them, spent a wonderful few years partying, living—*here, the actress

used air quotes with her fingers—*"alternative lifestyles,"* gener-
*ally having a good time on drugs, and then gone on to actually make*
*something of themselves, that in the years between their fun times and*
*their serious work they'd never, you know, like some people they*
*knew, bought a pressie on the street with fentanyl mixed in and died*
*before they could make something of themselves. I mean, those people*
*really are just jealous that their enemies have managed to live through*
*the tough cred-building years, not die, and then go on to artistic suc-*
*cess. How many people like that are dead now?* *Everyone knows*
*someone like that who weighs on them every time they have a moment*
*of success, who makes them think, oh god, I'm such an idiot for caring*
*about this, so-and-so would think I'm such a loser for this.* The actress looked down and tutted. *It doesn't even stand to think about*
*their attitudes,* she said, *because that entire group will be dead soon.*
*Of the people who became junkies so they didn't have to actually deal*
*with their ambitions, were any of them able to make it past thirty-five?*
she said. *And I mean, thirty-five is a stretch, because the age used to*
*be twenty-seven,* she said, *even with the added fentanyl from China,*
she said, raising her eyebrows. *They're lasting longer,* and she
looked up from her plate, the vegetables on which she had been
methodically rearranging, and she said, suddenly sotto voce, *you*
*know, I heard that sort of actress Rebecca Morris died,* she said. *She*
*was really something,* she said, *I heard that she had killed herself.*
She nodded slowly, glumly, and looked at Nicole, who was across
from her. *Wait*—her eyes bulged and she looked around at the
table—*was she a friend of yours?* She directed this at Nicole, who
had been nodding along with everything the actress said as she

sat at the dinner. Nicole nodded once again here, and the actress continued, now looking at Alexander, who was looking at the floor and shaking his head, *Oh god*—she put a hand to her mouth—*you were close with her, I'm so sorry. It is really too bad*, the actress said to Alexander. *I really thought she may have had some latent undiscovered talent*, she said. *You know, when I did a film with Netflix recently they wanted to hire some unknowns and I actually suggested Rebecca. I had seen her one-woman show or whatever it was she called it, and though it was obviously not the correct medium for her*—the actress paused to take a sip of wine and looked up as if she were formulating the correct way to say this—*it was clear that there was something appealing about her. She had a magnetism that was impossible to deny, but you could tell that she was addicted to squandering every opportunity that she had to make something of herself*, the actress said. *I used to audition for things with her once in a while, it was always so lovely to see her there in the room. She really stood out in Los Angeles. Like, that is not a Hollywood girl. She does not fit in in Hollywood. We didn't know each other well but she was always a friendly face to see in the room. She always had a sort of look of resignation even before her audition, it seemed like even before she got up and read her lines she knew she wasn't going to get the part. My guess is she clung too tightly to her conception of herself as a failure, as a broken person, and because of that I think she would subconsciously decide to throw the audition even before it started. We were all rooting for her*, the actress said, *all the other actresses I know who would see her at auditions, because you know, about fifteen people are all slotted together in the same folder in the casting director's office, the folder shows up at auditions together constantly*, the actress said. *Our whole little group, we were all rooting for her.* She took another sip of wine. *She should have become a director*, the actress said, *she reminded me so much of a wonderful director the way she knew how to manipulate people. You always wanted to do things for her without her even asking. She was very manipulative I noticed from just my few meetings with her*— manipulative *I mean as the highest compliment. She knew how to get what she wanted from people, which is the most important skill for a director. You know, a director I worked with on a limited series once told me that Kubrick said that directing is just knowing how to pick the best people and make them do your bidding. It was a shame that she was stuck acting and she couldn't adapt herself to what she was good at*, the actress said, *but you know what, that's the problem with so many actors. They have an idea of themselves as a static entity, a person of themselves, but that's a big mistake. They have to learn to be satisfied with being vessels for other people's ideas or else it will all go terribly. In a sense it is to your friend's credit that she couldn't break through*, the actress said, relaxing into her seat, allowing her body language to become larger, leaning forward and resting her elbows on the table as if she were playing a mafioso and the table was her desk. *Yes*, she repeated, *in a sense it is to your friend's credit that she was never able to break through. I sort of think my biggest asset as an actress is my vacuity. That's why it can be so fun doing big blockbusters where I'm just a piece of meat*, the actress said, smiling at Alexander. *I hope I get to do an even bigger one soon.* I watched as Nicole and Eugene nodded along to this. I'm

not sure why it surprised me that they were so willing, on the
day of Rebecca's funeral, to listen to some self-important C-list
actress call our friend a loser. I guess Rebecca was one in their
eyes, but I couldn't believe we were all sitting there listening to
someone who had just spoken about a film that I was sure would
recede into the endless scroll of streaming platforms as if it were
as important as the winner of the Palme d'Or, a person who had
just told us that she *would have helped Rebecca* get onto one of the
thousands of forgettable films made every year by billion-dollar
studios, content farms, as if we should all be so grateful to her for
*almost* making Rebecca's life *meaningful*, for *almost* making Rebecca's life amount to something greater than a tragedy, whereas
the real tragedy would have been if someone had harnessed Rebecca's intelligence to make a stupid film like the one the actress
was talking about, a film that would probably never even appear
in a theater—a film that mainly plays on mute in a dentist's waiting room or at best in the background, half-seen, to keep someone having a bout of nausea company as they retch into the toilet.
This was the kind of person for whom Eugene and Nicole held a
dinner so special that they could not cancel it because their friend
Rebecca had killed herself. But of course Rebecca was practically nothing to them while the actress was exactly the kind of
person that they were desperate to know. They needed people
like the actress because they had to prove to themselves that they
knew people outside of their cloistered New York City art world,
and so they issued invitations to whomever seemed important
enough to display to the rest of their parochial art world friends.

So often the outsiders would accept these invitations because they believed that to mix with these so-called art worldy people would bring them a kind of enlightenment or education that was *missing from their lives*, the proposition from Nicole and Eugene being that the invitee would open their own address book and allow these hosts to enter their social worlds, which of course never happened, as they could never conceal, even over the course of one evening, the scale of their monstrosity. The actress had returned to talking about the film that she was in with the canceled auteur, and from what I could tell she was defending it to Alexander, who had moved on from the point that the auteur's films glamorized wealth—as he sipped the Piper-Heidsieck cuvée brut that was now being poured—to criticize them for appealing to the lowest common denominator of society. He skipped defending Rebecca, not that I said anything either. The film producer, an unstoppable force of good nature, lifted one of his big fleshy fingers and said *Alexander, I know you're going to love our new film.* Alexander smiled wryly. He raised one eyebrow, a talent of his I had always been jealous of. *Oh?* The film producer misread Alexander's mocking tone for one of genuine interest. The producer's career had flourished because of his obliviousness to criticism, his forceful good nature, and his unwillingness to hear the word *no*, all of which contributed to his earned bad reputation with women. *Yes! You need to read the script*, the producer said. *I wonder what you'll think as a writer. It's about this book that's really cool. It's by this French guy Céline. Not very many people know about him, I think.* Alexander interrupted. *I know Céline.* The producer smiled. *Cool! Yeah, I figured you would. Daniel, the director, says it's just writers who know about Céline.* Alexander made a skeptical face that the producer ignored. *There's a book he wrote that has a part set in America called* The Long Day's Journey into Night. Alexander interrupted: Journey to the End of the Night. The producer smiled. *Right, yeah, the French translation can be different sometimes. Anyway, she*—here the producer waved his wineglass at the actress—*is maybe going to play this American nurse who the hero meets in the war and follows to New York. It's, like, a really deep book, about how life sucks.* Alexander put his head in his hands and without looking up said, *Yeah, okay.* The actress smiled. *Yeah, okay,* she repeated back to Alexander. *Yeah, okay,* she said again, more mockingly. *Look,* Alexander said, *I don't even particularly like Céline, he was a Nazi, for one, and usually dumb people who don't actually enjoy reading love that book in a sort of teenage goth way. Like, oh god, I'm so dark and twisted because I hate being alive, so I read such dark stuff.* The actress said that she really liked the book, the film adaptation of which, I realized, she was auditioning for at dinner. This may have explained her diatribe on literature, it was for the benefit of Eric, the producer. He was eating it up. Alexander conceded to the actress that *Céline was an interesting prose stylist, but since you're making a film out of the novel, how could any of the writing translate? I find it weird that that's the book you and that director guy felt the need to adapt, because what's interesting about it is its postmodern style, its deliriousness, but also I seriously doubt either of you will have anything particularly interesting to tell me even about the plot, given that the book is about the futility of even trying to have a nice life and all you seem to care about is making money by starring in digestible content for stupid people.* The producer put down his glass. *Whoa, man, you know that's not true!* Alexander shrugged and scrunched up his features, like he was trying to make his eyes and mouth meet his nose in the middle of his face. He exhaled. *I'm really happy for you that you're going to make a movie. I hope you guys have a nice time, and you even get the title right when you do it.* So, Alexander had begun to read books written in other languages. I was happy for him. The actress shook her head solemnly and raised her voice a bit. *Oh god, you're so pompous. You're really so annoying. Do you really think literature is some purist endeavor and everything else is stupid and evil? That writers lead intellectual lives and everyone else is an idiot, that even their readers are just consumers of their intellect unable to think anything for themselves, or even really engage with their work?* Alexander disagreed. *Of course not, people can engage with my work*, he said. *My work is quite easy to understand. But I don't want to talk to some sophomoric Hollywood people who think that by purchasing the rights to literature they have the right to interpret it, to make claims about it, to even say that they understand any of it.* The actress laughed. At this point Nicole was drinking heavily to distract herself, and shooting pleading, ineffectual looks at Alexander to make him stop talking. The actress, not noticing her hostess, said, *I think literally every novel, every so-called literary novel, is just as accessible as something like a pulpy paperback.* Alexander rolled his eyes. *No*, she continued, *I truly believe this. I see no difference between someone reading*

*Virginia Woolf and* Twilight, *I see no difference between Bolaño and Ferrante, and I think the people who need the categories, people who believe that by reading Proust they're geniuses, actually lock people out of having life-changing aesthetic experiences by acting like those things are harder to understand than they really are, and so they discourage so many people from ever picking up a book or going to the opera or seeing a piece of theater. That's why people don't just go to the bookstore and buy* Ulysses—*because people like you walk around like having been able to get through* Infinite Jest *was a heroic accomplishment rather than a pleasurable experience! Books are funny, books are a pleasure to read, art is meant to coax the viewer into a state of wonder and joy, and I think that we have lost that because now people think that reading is meant to be a solemn affair, and I mean, to some degree that's the fault of a literary establishment that only seems to be interested in publishing trauma porn, and authors are competing with one another to see who can write the most horrifically sad tale. Our Céline movie will be dark, but I wanted to work on it because I read the novel and I also found it hysterically funny. That's why it's such a great failing that literature these days has become so incredibly banal, so fixated on worthlessly depicting the mundane thoughts that their authors have as they drink a cup of coffee and mourn that their lives aren't more special. They've given us in Hollywood a monopoly on joy and humor and wonder. And those novelists who write in the most banal, truly meaningless diaristic style are often the snobbiest ones! The ones who believe that their work is more important, more virtuous, different in its very nature to the work that people actually enjoy. I think the snobs who believe the things they like deserve to exist more than the things that other people like are far more the destroyers of art rather than the so-called middlebrow public.* At this moment I began to like the actress, even though I essentially disagreed with so many things she said. Perhaps it reflects poorly on me that the only thing it takes to buy my approval is the ability to make my enemies upset, but the way that Alexander looked, sitting across from me at the long wooden table, the face that the actress was able to draw from his long and dour features, his little black eyes squinting in rage and embarrassment, was enough to make me positively giddy. Perhaps she did know who he was, it seemed as though she had read his novels, his long accounting of the unfairness of his life. Alexander here tried once again to interject, he raised his long, hairy pointer finger no doubt in order to defend what she called *boring lifeless fiction that depicts only the pathetic life of its author,* which made the whole exchange even more delicious, and I wondered if the actress was aware of the fact that she had set up a debate in which he had to defend himself on those terms. *I am a writer who describes my boring life!* She did not let him interrupt, though I wish she had, to see how he could explain his novel about two friendless men in Brooklyn who ran a failing laundromat, but instead she continued. *Look, man, I went to college, I was an English major! I read some pretty dense things. And even if I didn't I don't see why you have such a low opinion of your audience. Part of the reason I wanted to be an actress was because I loved stories, showing people stories. And I've tried to show people that the things I make are for everybody. Shakespearean drama is for the masses, and the things that intimidate people really shouldn't intimidate them at all, because all that they are, all that any art is, is something that another human being came up with. A human being who took baths, and ate spaghetti, and wrapped presents for their friends and family. That's what we should really understand about art. Because the extremely high art begs you to remember exactly that. High art reminds us of our humanity, not only of the intellectual prowess of its author. The thing that bothers me even more than people thinking reading is dead, that theater is dead and that Hollywood films killed it and therefore all Hollywood films are useless capitalist trash, because there is a bit of truth to that, what bothers me even more than that are the people that act like being intellectual is the most difficult thing of all, and that by reading and thinking and writing they are some kind of partisan force that exists outside of the general public. In addition to her novels and, like, inventing second-wave feminism or whatever, Simone de Beauvoir wrote about how she and Sartre had so much fun going dancing! The difference with these people is that they had real contributions to make to intellectual life and so they weren't worried about seeming frivolous, they knew that they didn't have to turn the mundane practicalities like hanging out with their friends into some kind of mythic performance of their intellects because nothing about their intellect was being called into question. But now, and I think it's because people aren't sure whether or not they're making real interventions, they find the need to turn everything into such a performance. I mean, why did you invite me here tonight to your cultural evening, as I think you described tonight on the invitation, when it's been one of the most culture-less evenings of my life, when all I've heard conversation about is travel itineraries and gossip and clothing and wine?* Here, she laughed and winked at the film producer, who was staring at her smiling. She really never stopped auditioning, and that was part of the great perversity of her character, which accounted for the success of her career. *You know, I was actually nervous to come here,* the actress said, *because I had seen one of Eugene's shows and I really didn't understand it, though I thought that I enjoyed it. But I thought there was something deeply intelligent about it that I couldn't understand and so I thought when I got the invitation to the dinner that there would be people who knew more than me about literature and art and music, and that I wouldn't be able to keep up with the conversation. I mean, I thought that I would say something foolish and everybody would laugh at the ridiculous Hollywood actress who didn't know the name of a Czech film director or the avant-garde composer, and I'm sure that there are people here who know more than me about those things, but from the way that this alleged cultural evening has played out, what I really should have been worried about was how boring it would be.* I looked around at the faces of my dinner companions. Nicole was slightly slack-jawed, awed by the rudeness coming from the actress's tidy, unintimidating, small frame. I noticed that I was laughing, smiling at the actress, almost creepily. I turned my eyes to the floor, mostly to hide myself from the consequences of openly supporting what she was saying, namely being addressed by Alexander or either of the monstrous couple who were our *hosts. To think I almost didn't come because I was intimidated,* she said, laughing. *I came to discuss ideas but instead I feel like a pilgrim who has walked for weeks only to find his holy site littered with trash and covered in graffiti. Talk about Ozymandias. I mean, really I feel like I've been slapped in the face by the inanity of your conversation. I feel for your friend Rebecca, I wonder what she would have been like if she were here. I wish I got to know her better. I'm sure she was nothing like you. From what I've gleaned, you guys in the art world need to elevate everything to make it feel worthwhile. Why not just admit to enjoying a beautiful object, instead of finding the need to justify it to yourself by discussing it in unintelligible language that doesn't describe why you like it? I actually remember our host here introduced himself to me as an explorer of the performance of objects, which confused me and made me feel stupid, but was part of what made me want to come to this dinner. I now realize it was obviously a meaningless way of saying he enjoys being rich and having nice things, though I'm not sure, given his conduct tonight, that he particularly enjoys anything aside from red wine.* I couldn't hold back my laughter, and I could see Eugene look up and sort of glower at me, and then look the same way at the actress, who he had clearly at one point believed he was going to have sex with, instead had just called his artistic practice—his entire life really—stupid and boring and *bad for the world.* I could see him purposefully looking down at his plate, either because the actress had just made him feel deservedly ashamed or perhaps because he was quite drunk at this point and, like a yoga *drishti,* he was using his plate as a focal point to harness the power of his mind to keep himself from throwing up his sunchoke soup. Nicole without my noticing it had absconded to hide in the kitchen because she could hear her husband being ripped to shreds by the woman she thought would become her friend and bring her along to an entirely new set of galas than the galas she was already invited to, or maybe she had just gone to the kitchen to pretend to be involved in the preparation of the meal. She returned, the clacking of her clogs against the floor alerting everyone to her entrance, and her strange attempt at a smile, her nostrils deeply flared, which made it look a bit like she were smelling nail polish remover, announced that it was time for everyone to put on cheery faces. She was carrying a gilt tray of marzipan fruits in unnatural colors, another one of her specialties *de la maison*. I always found it delightful to look at these surrealist treats: perfectly sculpted strawberries rendered in blue with orange seeds, miniature white pears, ombré red bananas. She set the tray down beside me and smiled. I felt warmly toward her against my better judgment, against my will. I must remember not to get drunk and start feeling things, I thought, sat at the dinner table. Whenever I have a few sips of *natural wine*, wine that is actually oversweet and tastes like it's been filtered through a hay bale, I begin to start *feeling things* against my control, I begin to *soften* the defenses that I so *clearly* need to maintain against people like Nicole's charms—charms that in her case are so clumsy, are so basic, that I begin to feel love for everyone, like a ridiculous coward. Really, I begin to question my morals completely once I've had a glass or two of wine. I think that if I were to be in a room with Josef Mengele, if he were to supply me with some quality white wine, dry with a high mineral content, I would probably be toasting to his tenacity, his aptitude for scientific achievement, his perseverance and determination in the face of less-than-ideal research conditions. I smiled at Nicole as she put the tray down next to me. Though I loved the look of the fruits she always bought from some secret sugarmonger in Queens, I never ate the marzipan because I found it grainy and overly sweet. Had Nicole remembered that I hated the taste of marzipan and put it next to me to taunt me? Or had she put it there because she remembered that I loved the way that the little blue peach-shaped marzipan looked? I was beginning to bore myself with my deep-seated hatred of Nicole. I really needed to leave this apartment before I drove myself insane on the hamster wheel of detesting them, then feeling sorry for them, then feeling remorseful both about detesting them and feeling sorry for them. How boring. And of course it was at that moment that Eugene took me out of my indulgent circular thoughts. *Nicole, you ass*, Eugene shouted with his body draped over the young artist's shoulders as if he were the python Britney Spears danced with as a shawl at the VMAs. *Nicole, you are so boring. Nicole, bring those over here. Nicole, you are so tedious, bring me those.* Nicole pretended not to hear Eugene, and suggested, speaking directly to the actress, that everyone move away from the dining table for dessert and sit on the sofas, which was a welcome idea, as I did love my seat on that white sofa, but the thought of returning to the sofa made me a bit sick, it would feel like going backward in time to the beginning of this dreadful evening, an invitation to do it all again from the start. *Go, go*, Eugene shouted in reply, *go recline, you cow, but bring me those stupid things.*

Eugene was now laughing into the shoulder of the young artist, who was trying to pry his arms off her. I could faintly hear Nicole whispering at her husband to stop shouting, she was doing that kind of show whisper where the audience was meant to hear everything that the quarreling leads were pretending to conceal. *You are humiliating yourself*, she hissed at Eugene, and then she turned toward the actress's seat and bent down to her seated level, creating an intimacy between the two of them while speaking loud enough for Eugene and everyone else to hear, and said to the actress *he only gets like this when he's had a bit too much to drink, it really is harmless*, and then she stood up and sweetly said to her husband *it would be best if you took yourself to bed*. At this point Eugene stood up and announced that he would not like to go to bed, but that he would rather like to dance, that he felt a lot like dancing, and so he got up from his chair and went to Nicole and took both of her arms and started dancing her around the room, dragging her body around the room. Eugene, who was a full head shorter than *his partner*, was powering her through the big open space of the loft. The twinkling lights of the city in the large glass windows behind them would have been the perfect backdrop to a romantic evening in which a couple, very much in love, couldn't help but dance in front of their dinner guests. *Those two just can't keep their hands off each other*, I thought, chuckling softly to myself. Nicole's angry, squished-up face relaxed into an expression of resigned boredom as her husband dragged her around, barely missing a large papier-mâché sculpture next to one of the windows. Nicole's fitted purple tube skirt prevented

her from taking strides that matched his, and he was dragging
her around at such a pace that she had to move her feet at a quick
pitter-patter that made her look more eager to participate than
she really was. She freed one of her hands from his and hit him
on the top of his bald head, commanding him to stop, as he
grinned wildly and marched her back toward the table where
everyone was sitting, dumbfounded, watching their hosts' *pas de
deux*. This was the real Eugene in action. Many people at the
dinner were made visibly uncomfortable by Eugene's transfor-
mation into the rumba king, especially the young people at the
dinner who I didn't know and who clearly were not as used to
this kind of behavior from their host, whereas I could see that
across the table Alexander was suppressing a smile because he
too knew this behavior so well. It depressed me to group myself
and Alexander as the *veteran camp* of Nicole and Eugene dinners,
but it was the truth that we knew that the price of attendance at
Eugene's house was watching him drunkenly abuse his live-in
victim. One wondered why Nicole allowed him to do this, allowed him to continue not only to sponge off of her financially
but also destroy every effort she made to social-climb out of
their *little set* of the *faithful* and into the greater cultural world, a
world beyond a small neighborhood made up of ten to fifteen
city blocks. Alexander stood up and, like a child who continues
to play with his toy soldiers as Mommy and Daddy throw home
furnishings at one another, made his way to the living room,
where we had all been sitting before dinner. The actress and
Clara Carson and the young people followed him, and I watched

as the young female artist around whom Eugene had been wrapped threw a sort of hesitant look toward Eugene and then turned her head toward everyone, and then to the ground, as if to say *please don't associate me with his actions*, before following the others to the living room as Eugene dragged Nicole around the loft in a polka-style dance. It was hard to feel as sorry for Nicole as she would have liked you to. Of course, it's detestable to blame a woman for her partner's deranged, disturbed, and disgusting conduct, but in the case of Nicole and Eugene it was clear that this conduct was the very heart of their relationship— that unlike in the situation of most *abused women*, Nicole was the one that held the power in their relationship; Nicole was the one with millions of dollars' worth of art, jewelry, property, and cash, and though Eugene was the owner of their jumbo loft, he could in no way afford the lifestyle he was accustomed to without Nicole. He could pretend that his artistic bona fides were the reason they stayed at the Gritti during the Venice Biennale, that the trips to Mexico and the Bosporus were treats he put on for his *studio assistants*, that the house in Rhinebeck was his idea, his property, but really Eugene knew that Nicole paid for all of these things, that without Nicole he couldn't afford the taxes on his loft *and* the house upstate *and* the trips to the seaside with his *studio assistants*. Perhaps he could afford some of these material delights on his own, but without them *all* he wasn't sure that life was worth living, and so he was at the mercy of Nicole and her money. And yet Nicole was willing to allow him to drag her bloated body, as rigid and lifeless as her Botoxed forehead,

around their home. Perhaps she loved being made to feel powerless and small. Perhaps that was what Eugene had over her, why
Eugene had captured her, still, after all these years, when he
dragged her body around their home—that even though she
stood a head taller than him he made her feel so wonderfully tiny
and weak. Meanwhile I was back sitting in my old friend, the
corner seat of the sofa, once again regretting my decision to
come here, back to the Bowery, where so much of my extreme
youth was spent. I looked at the young artist across from me who
had spent the night being felt up by Eugene and I remembered
how I had felt so humiliated here, in the Bowery, in fact I felt at
this very moment so very humiliated and, of course, in the Bowery, I didn't need to remember anything because it was as it always was. Yes, I was watching Nicole and Eugene and feeling
humiliated in the Bowery just exactly as I had been years before.
We think that we change and grow but actually nothing in our
lives ever changes even a little bit. People are obsessed with saying *every ten years all the cells in your body have regenerated*, that
every ten years your body works to rid itself of all that it is, to
become something new, that *you are an entirely new person every
ten years*, but people do not understand that, for these new cells to
herald a complete shift in your being, you would need to shelter
them, and yourself, from whatever toxins you were trying to get
rid of in the first place—that in the same way that only after ten
full years of not smoking do we possess a body that has never
smoked, if we continue to frequent the same places that ruin us
we will never change, and so often whatever cells we shed are

left as dust in the seat where we remain for another decade, I thought as I sat once more in the corner seat of the sofa at Eugene and Nicole's house on the Bowery. As we endeavor to change, we sit molting in the same places, so that by the time we're meant to be *brand-new* all those squeaky-clean cells have been sullied by the same surroundings we've been trying so hard to slough away. Eugene, who had finally relaxed his grip on his wife, sat in a chair across the room feeding himself cocaine from a key. The actress, who was sitting on an uncomfortable wrought iron chair I'd always thought Eugene and Nicole had bought as a torture device, struck up a conversation with the young artist, who had wrested herself from Eugene's grip. The young artist who had been sitting with Eugene throughout the dinner suddenly looked as if she had switched on. Her vacant face was replaced by the look of someone listening intently. The young artist had told the actress that she had only moved to New York a few months ago, that she was enjoying all the wonderful people she'd met since leaving Miami, a culture-less place full of beautiful people, for New York, which had just as many beautiful people, but people who at least seemed like they were *interested in things*. She disagreed with the actress that everyone in New York was as vacuous and terrible as she'd said they were. She had made great friends here, found an audience for her work, found people to talk to. The actress bent over and rested her elbows on her legs, which were spread wide on her chair as if she were a high school football coach about to inspire his team to make a sudden comeback. *Y'know*, the actress said, *I hope that's how you'll feel forever.*

*When I moved to LA,* the actress said, *I thought my life was about to change in a really beautiful way. I had this idea that I was going to be surrounded by people who were interested in the same kinds of things as I was. Suddenly I had access to the world of culture. There were art galleries, and great movie theaters and restaurants I'd read about in the newspaper. For the first few months I spent all my free time, when I wasn't going to auditions or working as a nanny, driving around the city, going to poetry readings, walking around the fancy neighborhoods where every bit of nature felt so domesticated, so groomed and artificial, the streets smelled of roses. I was intoxicated by the feeling that I was no longer on planet earth but rather in Los Angeles. But after a few months of awe, I realized that I missed my old life because what I missed more than anything was openness. I missed people who were willing to admit they didn't know things, that they had never heard of things, that they were open to learning about new things, people who weren't*—here the actress looked around at the people sitting in the living room—*so incredibly blasé about everything. Sometimes,* the actress said, swirling around the ice in the pea Collins glass, *sometimes I get messages online from friends from high school telling me how amazing my life looks, and how proud they are of me, and how much they wish they could trade their mundane everyday existences living in the suburbs of Denver where we grew up, how bland and settled everything is there, taking care of their kids and looking after their husbands, maybe working boring jobs. But sometimes,* the actress said, *sometimes I just look at their profiles for hours, clicking through their photos, looking at pictures of their kids, a trip to the lake, a birthday barbecue, and I think they all look so boring and middle-aged and bland and happy, so so happy, and they're all smiling in the photos, big, unrestrained, toothy smiles. I mean, sometimes I'm happy with my friends but none of us are ever smiling in photos, I mean, we're all pulling these faces meant to accentuate our jawlines, doing the skinny arm, and I look at my friends' pictures and I think, I wish just a little bit that that were me, I mean, I look at the kinds of people I have to associate with now*—here she physically gestured at Eugene—*and I think, well, it's either these rich so-called interesting people or it's fans or it's other famous people so that we can all feel okay and safe, insulated from interacting with people who might be too excited to see us*—*I mean, can you believe how much of my life is devoted to protecting myself from people that are too excited to see me? And I know they don't really care about me and that all it means really is that I am a part of their personality and they want some externalized manifestation of their personality and so meeting me and taking a photo closes a feedback loop for them. Actually, it tends to be pretty disappointing for them, because meeting someone you know from TV doesn't mean you immediately get to experience the intimacy you have with their character. The people in my life who are most excited to see me are strangers, who don't know me at all and feel a bit let down once they actually do meet the real me. Obviously it's pathetic to complain about celebrity, and it's even stupider to yearn for an authentic-seeming life, I mean, it's no better than the rich people who have nothing better to do than have babies and build nice houses for themselves and post about it online and think that this is somehow interesting. As if being able to afford a nice tasteful life is somehow an achievement! As if it's groundbreaking to wear a pretty dress and be in nature and hold a baby. But sometimes I so wish I could have been like one of the people I used to know when I was younger in Colorado. I could own a boutique like my friend Angela, and sell clothes that have nothing to do with what's on the runways, pretty, simple, obvious dresses that make regular women feel beautiful.* I started to feel bad for the actress. Her life must be incredibly bleak to engage in these middle-class everywoman fantasies that revolved around some nostalgic American being-in-common that no longer existed even for her parents' generation. Next I imagined she'd start talking about white picket fences and apple pies and square dancing in the town hall. Perhaps show business had taught her that ludicrous bathos was the height of style. She was still talking. *I could chat with my customers, who I would know, who I would watch grow up, whose daughters I would order prom dresses for, women who would take me with them to pick out wedding dresses, we would all be a little group in the shop and we would all talk over our problems and they would invite me to their weddings like the hairdresser Dolly Parton in* Steel Magnolias, *and I would see some of the guests wearing outfits I sold to them, and we would wink at each other when their husbands said they looked so effortless because we both remembered the torment of finding something that flattered their shape and didn't upset the bride's color scheme. I would get to be a part of the intimate lives of so many women for whom a special occasion, wearing a beautiful dress, was a highlight of their year rather than a weekly red-carpet slog. I could help people feel better about themselves. Maybe the real problem is that I'm so busy trying to prove to myself that I'm a success, trying to act out*

the kind of person I feel like I'm supposed to want to be, that I've totally forgotten who it is that I ever wanted to become. Alexander
laughed. Alexander, throughout her speech, was fuming in his
seat on the sofa, and the actress occasionally flashed him a jackal's smile. *You're so hopelessly bourgeois*, he said, *you're so hopelessly bourgeois that after a few years of even living in a world of the
dregs of culture you're intellectually burnt out and ready to return to
your simple parochial town, to watch television and run a clothing
store. Good for you, self-knowledge is important. I don't know why
you think yourself an authority on art or literature when the things
that you make are brainless and repellent. Have your creative choices
left you feeling empty? No wonder*, Alexander said. *No wonder.* The
actress relaxed into her seat and laughed, eyeing Alexander, ad-
justing the buttons of her little blazer. *Oh god, enough! I've had
enough of you. You pretend to be so serious about things*, she said,
*when really you're just insecure and boring so the only interesting
thing you can do is be vicious toward everyone.* Alexander leaned
back and laughed. *No really*, the actress said, *you're disgusting.
You think your look of disdain and superiority is hidden, but it's been
plastered across your face all night.* Alexander shrugged a bit. The
actress shook her head. *I don't need to show you that I'm better than
you because I know that you make yourself suffer every day all on your
own. People like you are the worst kind of people. You do a disservice
to art just by being related to it.* Alexander laughed. *I'm not kidding.
You're one of the most unkind people I've ever met, but I don't blame
you. I don't like you, I find you incredibly unpleasant, I don't want to
be around you. Your attitude makes the best part of being alive seem*

*like an impossible, distant, and remote thing reserved for only the most brilliant people. You act like all you want to do is have serious conversations about art and about literature, and that only a select group of people who have studied enough, who have the credentials you think are important, are smart enough to engage with you, but what is even inside of a book but people's thoughts and feelings? Everyone can understand thoughts and feelings. Everyone can read a book and understand it. Maybe it's because you find life so hard to navigate that you think the human experience is difficult to understand. It makes sense because you're all total nonentities. You don't even figure into life. You're all total nonentities.* Alexander scoffed. Eugene started laughing, and shouted *burn it all down, baby,* and the actress rolled her eyes. *I really don't want to be around any of you, I wouldn't have come to this dinner if I knew this is what you'd be like. I should never have come here. People think that these Manhattan evenings with beautiful views and intelligent conversation are what make life worth living. Maybe they are, and we just haven't had one tonight.* The actress as punctuation crossed her legs, though in a somewhat cumbersome way because they were constrained by the pink bouclé tweed, and now I was really laughing, laughing out loud, and tears were coming to my eyes because I was *grateful,* so *grateful* that the actress—for whom this meeting with Alexander was meaningless—had done me such a wonderful service, I was grateful for what she had done. I had never been able to speak to him this way because it would appear only like the words of a regretful lover, of a jealous contemporary, but the actress had no ties to Alexander and so she could have at him remorselessly, she had seen the bullshit at the center of this tweed-wrapped barbarian and she hadn't let him get away with it, and although her attack on him wasn't as precise as I'd have been, in a sense her passionate outburst was much better than anything I could ever have said because it left my hands completely clean. Yes, the actress had no idea of the depths of what was *really* wrong with Alexander, but in a way, her words would ring truer because they were uncoated with the malice of former friendship. The problem with Alexander and Eugene and Nicole was not their destruction of art but their destruction of all those who allowed themselves into their orbits, their bloodsucking, and she had been able to identify that about all of them on first glance. Perhaps she was wiser than I. At first, before I had met her, I had despised the actress for coming and trampling all over the memory of Rebecca, then I had, in an unintentional alliance with Alexander, been uninterested in her because she starred in boring films with no aesthetic or intellectual value, but now, as Alexander stood up and began to stomp out of the loft, it came over me that I actually loved the actress, that whatever she played in, even if it was a television soap about CIA agents falling in love with each other and killing people, I would watch and think *that is my ally, that is my friend.* The actress was right, they were all total nonentities. I knew this already but no one had ever spoken it so plainly. People called them disgusting, stupid, exploitative, but never *nonentities.* They were successful and well-known enough not to be discounted but that didn't stop them from being *nonentities.* But Eugene and Nicole, even Alexander, were total

*nonentities*, so why was I still identifying with them? Why had I
carried them around in my psyche like a heavy water bottle I'd
forgotten about in a hidden pocket of my luggage and schlepped
around to three different continents? I realized I had hated them
so much because I felt like I was one with them. I had felt like the
world was incredibly small and they were its center, and even
when I left for Europe I was still hiding out from them because it
was *their world*. Theirs was the legitimate world and I was in
exile. As many people as I met, people who knew them, people
who hated them, people who didn't know who they were, it still
felt that way. But it wasn't true, these people were *total nonentities*, people I was completely free to leave. Because I hadn't seen
them since I'd slunk away like a naughty dog, it was like they
were still waiting, my leash and collar ready for my return. With
each lacerating comment from the actress I felt their claim on me
was weakened until suddenly I was just totally free. Oh, goodbye. I was my own person, a real person, who had nothing to do
with them. The actress wasn't speaking *to me*, and I realized it
was because I had nothing to do with *them*. I had nothing to do
with these people. But because in my mind Nicole and Alexander
and Eugene *were* New York, and I was practically gestated in the
off-brown juices of the Hudson River, it felt like I was sullied
from the start. I had no choice but to be like them. Of course, it
took me time to find them, but when I did it felt like this was the
place I was destined for. It was inevitable, this was who I was,
and it was garbage. But the actress was willing to make herself
over, to think about the lives of her old friends without letting

them define her. Sure, what she'd remade herself into was of no interest to me, but she clearly wasn't a fugitive from them in her own life. They were *nonentities*. The jackals in this loft hadn't created me, they had no ownership over me, they were *nonentities*. I actually pitied them the way that the actress secretly pitied her friends who she looked at on Facebook. What quaint lives. What thwarted little lives. I smiled. Nicole, who had been sitting silently, frozen, following the proceedings like a tennis spectator, apologized to the actress. *I think emotions are running high because of the traumatic loss we've all just suffered. The death has cast a pall over the evening.* Eugene started cackling. *Yes, sweetheart, it is inconvenient Rebecca died, it has given the whole night a sort of bad vibe.* Nicole stamped her foot. *You know that's not what I mean.* Alexander took this display of emotion as his cue to actually say his goodbyes. He was hovering near the door waiting for anyone to register that he'd stormed away, and, because no one had, he used Nicole's outburst as a way to save face and creep back into the fold. He moved silently toward Nicole and gave her a tight, long hug, a distasteful hug about Rebecca, all the while glowering at the actress over Nicole's shoulder. He then shot a not-very-nice look at me, and once again swaggered away, this time ruining the drama of his silent goodbye as he knocked over something loud and wooden while fumbling with his coat in the closet. The actress smiled to herself and began to stand up slowly, not to follow him but to watch his departure. It was the act of a cowboy who has driven the bandits out of town, she had vanquished the enemy not because the villagers deserved her help but simply because that's *what the cowboy does*. In fact, judging by the look on her face, she resented feeling that by ousting Alexander she had grouped herself in with the people assembled around Nicole and Eugene's living room. She wasn't a villager. It was time for her to ride off into the sunset. Nicole followed after the actress and grabbed her by the wrists. *You have to stay*—she was struggling to come up with a reason—*maybe Eugene will show us some of his new work for his show at the Kunstverein Hannover.* Even Nicole wasn't sold on her own excuse, and she dropped the actress's wrists as she said it, resigned to watching her walk out of the house. *She's leaving because I won't share the BLOW!* Eugene said, holding himself up just barely on the ottoman. Much to my, and everyone's, surprise, however, the actress swiveled on her heels and came to sit back down in the living room, lowering herself back onto the wrought iron torture chair in a grand theatrical gesture. Nicole tried to rouse her husband from the ottoman but of course Eugene wasn't going to be showing anybody anything aside from his limp body and, if we stayed here long enough, his soiled trousers. The young artist was giggling to herself now, as if she had suddenly become the actress's accomplice, and the actress, perhaps recognizing the disloyalty of the young artist to her hosts and finding it distasteful, asked the young artist what was so funny. Nicole answered instead, and said *you have a beautiful laugh*, patting the knee of the young artist in a maternal way. The young artist smiled. Nicole addressed the actress, *don't you just love having younger people around, don't they just liven up the evening?* And the young artist said that she appreciated being *listened to* in a room full of such *interesting people*, even if they *couldn't get along* it was nice that they had *opinions about things*. The young artist's naïveté bothered me, not because I recognized a former version of myself in her, or because I regretted not being the *youth delegation*, but because she was proof of how low Eugene and Nicole had fallen. They were always on the hunt for some young blood to suck to keep themselves abreast of what was going on with young people and had usually been able to fill the post with young people who made up for their lack of worldliness and connections in originality and wit. Now, either Nicole and Eugene were unable to attract the aspirants they once could or, even worse, they had lost their ability to discern who was worth their investment. Actually, I realized, as I watched Nicole rub the young artist's arm, there was no doubt I once sounded exactly like that. There was no doubt I'd once seemed exactly as innocent and pliable and dumb, I'd just chosen to forget all about it because remembering it made me feel as sick as I did now. The actress smiled at the young artist. *Watch out*, she said, *because I have a feeling it's not just paintings our hosts expect from artists*. She turned to Nicole and smiled the smile that beat out all the other actresses in her drawer. *If it was a performance you were after this evening, I am glad I could have played my part*. My hero the actress left, and most of the others followed after her, either because the height of the drama was over or because it was true, Eugene would not share the blow. The young artist went back into the hallway, no doubt to find Eugene and his baggie, and I followed after her aiming to collect

my jacket, and in my effort to keep a distance between myself
and the young artist so it didn't seem I had followed her, I missed
the grand exodus of the rest of the party, and when I returned to
the main room I saw Nicole sitting alone on the sofa in the after-
math of her *cultural evening*. If being disappointed was a science,
Nicole was its Oppenheimer, a generational genius, forced to
suffer under the weight of her own achievements. I gave her a
strange little wave and a drunken smile, and I felt a bizarre compassion for Nicole bubble up in my stomach, Nicole trapped in
the perfectly terrible cage of her own creation, and then, feeling
that compassion turn to indigestion, remembering what had
happened the last time I was left alone with Eugene and Nicole,
I rushed toward the door. Nicole, ever the hostess, stood up and
intercepted me on my way out. *It was wonderful to see you*, I said
to Nicole, *thank you for having me*, I said, as she walked me to the
door, somehow the last person to leave the party. *I had a wonderful time*, I said, obviously lying, as Nicole looked quizzically at
me, returning my irony. I could tell that she did not believe me,
because though Nicole is an idiot she is not stupid, but even
though I'd made no effort to appear as though I was having a
nice time, for some reason it hurt me to see Nicole made so sure
of it, and because I am a great sufferer from a disease of the mind
whose major symptom is that I must be well-liked by all, even by
those I do not respect, in fact particularly by those I do not respect, I said to Nicole as I stood in the doorway of the floor-
through loft, *I'm back for a few months, let's do this again soon*. Not
only had I revealed too much of myself, but I had reintroduced

some kind of continuity to our relationship—I had allowed her
to feel as though I wanted her to be close to me, I had negated my
entire many yearslong endeavor of hiding from her and Eugene,
the thesis of which was to demonstrate that I wanted nothing to
do with them. I had essentially said to her, *my life without you is
not as wonderful, please take me back*, when my desired parting
sentiment was, goodbye, you disgusting leech, I wish never to
see you or your elegant hairstyle ever again, I regret my reac-
quaintance with your hideous vetiver oil drenched neck, a neck
I instead wrapped my arms around and embraced. Yes, instead I
said, *let's do this again soon*, instead I let her know that I was *back
for a few months*, that we had all the time in the world to resume
our old intimacy. Nicole looked at me with what I think was supposed to be puzzlement, but it was hard to tell with her because
of the way her immovable forehead made her look like she was
always slightly startled. *Yes*, she said, *that would be nice.* Then
because I'm a moron I said *Rebecca would have loved this*, and then
I stepped away from her and let the large metal door slam behind
me. A satisfyingly final noise, that great heavy door that I imagined could cut through bone, severing whatever ties remained
between me and the life on the Bowery I used to have. And I
raced down the stairs, taking them two at a time, my long black
skirt stretching out between each step, slightly encumbering my
drunken black avalanche down the stairs. I felt somewhat manic
and allowed myself to fly into the front door. I pushed out of the
apartment building and was met with the soot-colored colon-
nade of the Bowery, where just two days ago I had paced up and

down trying to reclaim my mind after it was intruded by terrible
thoughts about Rebecca's death, and I was drunk now, beautifully drunk, and the freedom that came with the dark sky, the
cold air, the tall buildings that ran along the Bowery and allowed
me to feel nestled in, hemmed in by the beaux arts architecture,
swaddled as I walked up and down the Bowery, and I considered
getting a cab home, back to my grandmother's apartment uptown, but the thought of being confined to a taxicab did not appeal to me, no, my legs felt strong, like they were desperate to be
used to carry me as far away as possible from that meeting with
Eugene and Nicole and Alexander, from that life that I had once
had, from the wake for Rebecca absent of any thoughts of Rebecca, where I had allowed myself to be complicit in Eugene and
Nicole's barbarism, had even allowed someone else to be their
victim in my presence, and there was a beautiful silence that
night, and I found my legs carrying me down the Bowery, I felt
myself following some kind of magnetic pull down the Bowery,
of course in the opposite direction of my home, speed walking,
almost running down the Bowery, the wide-open horizon and
the beautiful silence propelling me to almost run, and I couldn't
tell if I was running away from something or toward something,
if the life in New York that I was trying so hard to escape was
pulling me toward its very center, toward Rebecca's apartment,
toward where I used to live above the all-night video game café
when I had managed to get myself out of Nicole and Eugene's
and into my own apartment, and I had tried so hard to leave New
York, the city of my birth, my city, the best city, my beloved

New York, but really all I wanted to do was to escape the people within it, and ever still they were the center of my world, and my mind was empty as I ran as fast as I could, panting, and suddenly I realized I had begun to meditate, something I had never done until a few months before I returned to New York and I had begun practicing a form of meditation that a yoga teacher taught me, and there was an advertisement for a yoga class on the beach and I attended it because I had hurt my wrist from repetitive strain while typing, and I was the only student in the class and so after a period of stretching and strengthening my wrist the yoga teacher decided to do some kind of guided meditation and had me lie down and put her hands on my face and said in that strange Balkan accent *you think no good thoughts*, she said that she could tell that I was rolling my eyes secretly at everything that happened to me, and that this was not a way to pass through life happily or meaningfully but instead this was a way to guarantee I experienced no pleasure, no happiness, no intimacy, even with myself, and I resented this assessment from the yoga teacher, who was a white person with thick dreadlocks, but in resenting the assessment I realized that of course she was right, and she taught me a meditation that she said was invented at Stanford by psychologists, and of course because I am an idiot of exactly that type this legitimized the meditation, this meditation being one where I was meant to think happy thoughts about someone who I thought needed them, she told me to send good wishes with my mind, happiness and love, toward whoever I wanted to be happy, to allow the first person I thought of into my mind and wish happiness and love for them, and so without even hesitating I thought of Rebecca, who I hardly ever thought about and hadn't spoken to for so long, but who I always wished happiness and love for because no one else needed so much love and lacked so much happiness, and I pictured Rebecca's big almond eyes, her dark hair, and thought *I wish you love, I wish you happiness, I wish you love, I wish you happiness* and I remember that after an unknown period of time wishing happiness and love the yoga teacher told me to open my eyes and I discovered that I was weeping, that tears were rolling down my face and I was weeping like a child, I wasn't even thinking of Rebecca anymore, I was just weeping thinking the phrase *happiness and love*, and I was absolutely horrified to see this *guru* with a satisfied little smile on her face, sure that she had enlightened me, but something truly changed within me hoping for happiness for Rebecca, and of course I had wished for happiness for Rebecca in the past, but the practice of sitting and begging the so-called universe to give it to her allowed something to change in myself, allowed me to understand that happiness was something that you sought yourself, something that the people around you could wish for you, that you could meet people, meet friends, for whom your CV, your qualifications, your money were less important than your desire for happiness and love, and so I ran down the Bowery, unburdened by all of them, and I thought *happiness and love* about Eugene, who was probably at this moment throwing up all over the young artist, I thought happiness and love about Nicole, who was likely micromanaging the cleaners in the great room of the loft in order to feel less alone while the *man of the house* was *preoccupied*, I thought happiness and love about Alexander, who was likely, like I was, rushing home to write about the evening in order to make sense of it all, and I wished them all a painless sleep, I wished for their removal from my life, and I wished a painful bout of syphilis for Eugene, I wished a catastrophic opening for Nicole, I wished for another tepidly reviewed book for Alexander, but I wished them all happiness and love.

# NOTE ON *WOODCUTTERS*

*Happiness and Love* took as its starting point Thomas Bernhard's 1984 novel, *Holzfällen*, translated into English as *Woodcutters*. When I first read the novel, I was struck by how much Bernhard's artistic world in Vienna reminded me of my own. An ocean and forty years separate our novels, but I saw something I, regrettably, recognized in his vapid, transactional, louche pseudo-intellectual crowd. Soon after finishing *Woodcutters*, I began to take apart its structure and seat my own reprobates around the dinner table.

I riffed off the original shape of *Woodcutters*, a run-in, a funeral, a dinner party, but I allowed my players to explore new, horrible horizons in *Happiness and Love*. And indeed, both novels share a climax, though I think my optimism at the end of the book strangely, comes from having read Bernhard, literature's favorite misanthrope. There he was, sat on the wing chair, angry about the same things I am. Things aren't uniquely bad now, because there never was a golden age, when all the right things were recognized, and there will always be at least someone who agrees with you. Reading *Holzfällen* is not essential to understanding my book, but really, I can't recommend it enough.

Zoe Dubno, 2025

# ACKNOWLEDGMENTS

Thank you to my friends who read early drafts of the book, and gave me suggestions, edits, inspiration, and encouragement. Teddy Dubno, Danielle Michaud, Davidson Barsky, Jos Demme, Ellie O'Neill, Laurence Copson, Maya Binyam, Veronica Harrington, Jaquen Castellanos, Lexy Benaim, David Fishkind, Rachel Hahn Alex Zevin, Hadley Walsh, Clementine Ford, Zoe Hitzig, David Adler, Laura Adler, and Ben Noam.

I'd also like to thank my reading group, "saloon" (Aria Dean, Sam Kenswil, Alec Recinos, Alex Iadarola, Makayla Bailey) for dropping our usual course of readings to meet and talk about my book early on as if it were a real thing.

Thank you to Cindy Spiegel, Jesse Shipley, Jim Brooks, Jennifer Simchowitz, Sandy Zabar, Francoise Dussart, Steven Donziger, and Jennifer Walsh for the support, love, guidance.

Thank you to everyone I texted hundreds of times about their opinions on the book cover—Ed Fornieles, Charlie Fox, Aidan Zamiri, Sam Marion, Elizabeth Akant, Matt Copson, Caroline Polachek, Bolt Brown, Collin Fletcher, Ezra Marcus, Willa Nasatir—I hope you like it.

Thank you to Caroline Tompkins for my author photo.

Eunnam Hong and Lubov Gallery, thank you so much for your genius painting on the cover.

Thank you to Jamie Bonelli and to Ellen Hirsch for the care.

Without the support of the MFA program at Rutgers Newark, this book would not be possible. The great John Keene, who advised an early version of this book as a thesis, gave me the most incredible notes and guidance. Thank you also to Akil Kumarasamy and Alice Elliott Dark for the revisions and for the belief in me. And, of course, thank you to Shari Astalos, and Sanjay Agnihotri for showing me the few, but important, merits of New Jersey.

Thank you to my publicists Addie Gilligan and Millie Seaward and to Janique Vigier and Alexander Droesch for plotting and scheming.

Thank you to everyone at CAA, especially John Ash, an angel, the Strawberry Boy, for holding my hand so well, and my vegetarian agents Mollie Glick and Julie Flanagan, who took me to a steakhouse to make me feel valued. Thank you to Gabby Fetters and Jake Smith-Bosanquet for the world.

Sally Howe and Bobby Mostyn-Owen edited this book and made it so much better. Thank you both for your belief in me, your insight, and especially your patience. I wish you both happiness and love.

I want to thank Natasha Simchowitz, for being born eight hours before me, I think because it would be unfair to make me live in a world without her.

Thank you to my grandparents: Barbara and Jack, who make me feel like I can do anything I want to (and will call every day to check on the progress). To my Zeida, who made up hundreds of stories just for me. And to my Bubbe. We had the most fun.

Thank you to my brother, Teddy, and my parents, Dan Dubno and Lisa Bernstein. How lucky I am!!

# ABOUT THE AUTHOR

ZOE DUBNO is a writer from New York. She attended Oberlin College and has an MFA from Rutgers University, Newark. Her fiction has appeared in *Granta*, her nonfiction in *The New York Times Magazine*, *The New York Review of Books*, *The Guardian*, *The Nation*, *Vogue*, *BOMB*, and elsewhere. She lives in New York and London. *Happiness and Love* is her first novel.